THE SHADOW OF THE GALLOWS

When homesteader Ralph Bannister is murdered, Tom Steadman becomes the obvious suspect. After being found guilty and sentenced to be hanged, he seeks the help of Bellington's Private Detective Agency. Zachary Cobb and Neil Travis make the journey to Newberry — with only four days left to prove Steadman innocent. But Cobb's troubles begin before he and Neil even arrive in the town . . . It will take a great deal of blood and trouble before Bannister's real killer can be revealed.

Books by Steven Gray
in the Linford Western Library:

STEVEN GRAY

THE SHADOW OF THE GALLOWS

Complete and Unabridged

LINFORD
Leicester

Gloucestershire County Council

British Library CIP Data

Gray, Steven
The shadow of the gallows.—Large print ed.—
Linford western library
1. Western stories
2. Large type books
I. Title
823.9'14 [F]

ISBN 978–1–84617–661–6

Published by
F. A. Thorpe (Publishing)
Anstey, Leicestershire

Set by Words & Graphics Ltd.
Anstey, Leicestershire
Printed and bound in Great Britain by
T. J. International Ltd., Padstow, Cornwall

This book is printed on acid-free paper

1

'We must stand together and fight.'

With each word Ralph Bannister smashed one clenched fist into the palm of his other hand. At the same time he stared out at the twenty or so home-steaders gathered in front of him. He was a good speaker and he was pleased but not surprised to note that most were nodding in agreement.

Of course, Fred Warren looked even more worried than usual; would, if given the chance, voice caution, although it was doubtful many people would take notice. Silly old fool! Perhaps he was scared his sons would be in the fore-front of any fight. Looking at the boys' angry faces, the way they had taken to wearing holstered revolvers, Warren was probably right. Well, about Peter and David anyway. Martin, the sensible one, wouldn't want to be involved.

'Why should we let the cattlemen get away with molesting us when we ain't done nothing? Just because they've got might on their side don't mean they're goddamn right.'

Warren stepped forward. 'We should try talking to 'em.'

'Talking?' Bannister laughed loudly. 'Again? Where the hell is that goin' to get us? Where the hell has it ever gotten us in the past?'

'The law — '

Bannister interrupted. 'Law? What goddamn law? Marshal Jackson sits in his office and does nothing but bleat that as he's town marshal what happens outside the town ain't nothing to do with him. And you may be sure that if he should ever decide to get off his ass it'll be to take the side of the goddamn cattlemen.'

'You know that ain't true,' Warren objected.

'Ain't it?'

'Jackson is a good lawman. And we ain't never had trouble with the ranchers before . . . '

'Well, Fred, we sure as hell have got trouble now!' A chorus of yells and laughs greeted Bannister's words. After a while he held up a hand for silence.

'Or perhaps you didn't hear about the Pemberley boys? Farmers just like us. They were threatened by that bastard Steadman, beaten up by him and some of Rowlands' cowhands, and forced out of their homestead.'

'They were rustlers,' Warren said.

'So the goddamn Cattlemen's Association and their damn detective said. Where was the proof?'

'I didn't think proof was needed for something that everyone knows.' But looking round, Warren saw he was wasting his time.

There were one or two who agreed with him but their voices would also be lost because the rest wanted to go along with Bannister. Wanted action. Although what form that action would take he bet Bannister hadn't yet figured out. The man was good with words, good at rabble-rousing. He wasn't so good at thinking. He wouldn't take into consideration the fact that in any kind of a fight men on both sides risked getting hurt and that as the ranchers and their cowboys were in the majority the farmers would be the ones most at risk. Warren knew that if it came to a showdown the farmers could never hope to win.

Maybe later he'd ride round and talk to the others at their homes, try to get them to listen to reason. Glancing at his sons, Peter and David, he saw, with sinking heart, that they would be among the most difficult to persuade. For some while they'd been talking of little but what Bannister said and did. Hero-worshipped him almost. Had little time lately for their father, considering him timid and stupid, always ready to take what they saw as the coward's way out. They wanted to fight. And they might well take Martin along with them. Martin wouldn't start a fight but he wouldn't back down from one either, especially if his brothers were in danger of getting hurt.

Part of the trouble was Bannister was right. All of a sudden, instead of living side-by-side reasonably happily as they had done in the past, the ranchers did appear to be trying to drive the farmers out. For no good reason.

Of course when times were hard, farmers had always stolen a cow or two. The ranchers had mostly accepted it happened and turned a blind eye to it. Now they were using the likes of the Pemberleys, who were rustlers because that was easier than working on a farm, to call the rest rustlers as well. In this they were helped by Tom Steadman, the detective employed by the Cattlemen's Association. He had always been tough but fair, but now it seemed he was quite willing to use terror tactics in which he was supported by the Association.

'Can I count on you all?' Bannister's words broke into Warren's uncomfortable thoughts.

'Yeah!' The shout went up, echoing

round the field. One or two of the men even went so far as to draw and fire their guns.

This time Bannister didn't try to stop them sounding off. He was near the end of his speech and he wanted them to go away feeling angry and eager.

He waited until it was again quiet, before going on, 'Then I urge each and every one of you to keep your wits and your guns about you. Don't start a fight but be willing to finish one. Support and help one another. And that goes for every one of us!' He glared at Warren. 'If we act together we'll defeat the goddamn cattlemen. Make them respect and accept us! Because by God, we're here to stay!'

After more yells and cheers Bannister stood shaking hands as the homesteaders left the field. When they'd gone and he was alone he went over to his horse and swung himself up in the saddle. He was more than satisfied. It had been a good meeting, gone even better than he imagined it would. That old fool,

Warren, might attempt to persuade the rest to sit back and do nothing but he'd never succeed. The others were as impatient and furious as Bannister at the way the ranchers were riding roughshod over the farmers.

If it came to a war, and Bannister was sure it would especially if he had anything to do with it, then he had to make sure everyone was willing to do whatever it took to win. Make them realize he was protecting their interests as much as his own.

Because, he thought as he neared his farm, his interests were surely worth protecting.

His 160 acres were situated near to a waterhole which even in the hottest of summers didn't dry up completely. The crops he planted grew and thrived. He'd been here coming up for three years now and each year he made a larger profit. Because he spent most of his waking hours working on the land, his home might still be little more than a one-room shack but he'd already added a shelter for his animals and a corral. He'd started on a barn. It was hard work, sometimes a lonely life, but he wasn't about to give it up. Not for anyone.

He rode down the dusty slope through the sagebrush to the shack, looking forward to going into the cool and having a drink of lemonade. Talking was thirsty work and although still early in the year it was already hot, with no sign of the much needed rain.

As he dismounted, his horse flicked its head and whickered nervously.

'What is it?'

Then Bannister heard a noise from some way off. Alert for trouble he reached for the rifle in its saddle scabbard.

He never made it.

Even as he was drawing out the weapon something hit him, hard and painfully, in the chest. It was followed, an instant later, by the bang of a rifle. He was almost surprised to see blood spurting down the front of his shirt.

Christ, he'd been shot! It surely hadn't hurt that much to make such a mess. Before he could think of anything else the rifle was fired again and he was struck by a second bullet. His legs buckled under him and he fell to his knees. Grabbing at the wounds, he toppled sideways, everything went black and he lay still.

The dry-gulcher had no doubts that Bannister was dead. When he came out from his hiding place he saw that he was right.

2

As the jury filed back into the small and crowded courtroom a deep silence fell. The twelve men hadn't taken long to debate the case and reach their verdict and, with fluttering heart, Tom Steadman thought that boded ill for him. Especially as there had been plenty to speak against him and few to speak up for him

Judge Bowyer banged his gavel, more for effect than anything else as everyone was already quiet and waiting. He indicated that Steadman should get to his feet then turned to the jury. 'Well?' he demanded.

The jury foreman stood up. 'We find the defendant guilty of cold-blooded murder.'

Immediately the cowboys in the crowd started to jeer while the farmers cheered and there was a cry of 'Oh no,' from Amy Mallory.

'Quiet! Quiet!' Bowyer banged his gavel harder while Marshal Jackson stood ready to quell any unrest.

'And we reckon he should be hanged and real quick.'

When at last order was restored the judge said, 'Thank you, I don't need your advice on what sort of sentence to pass.'

Red-faced, the jury foreman sat down amidst some sniggering.

Bowyer turned to the prisoner. 'Mr Steadman, you have been found guilty after a fair trial and I have no hesitation in passing the death sentence on you. No one can be allowed to get away with murder just because the victim is a farmer and you are employed by the Cattlemen's Association.'

More jeers and cheering.

'Marshal.'

'Yes sir?'

'How long until a gallows can be built? And a hangman employed?'

'A week?' Jackson hazarded a guess.

'Yes, that sounds about right. So, Mr Steadman, seven days from now at a time to suit the marshal you will be taken from the jailhouse to the gallows and there hanged by the neck until you are dead. Court is over.' And with another bang of the gavel, Judge Bowyer stood up and left the room, pleased with the day's work. He never minded passing the death sentence on those who deserved it.

'C'mon, Tom, let's get you back to the jail,' Jackson said, stepping forward.

'I'm innocent you know that, don't you?' Steadman said, sounding both resentful and frightened.

'I don't know anything of the sort.'

Hand gripping his rifle, Jackson began to lead the prisoner out of the courtroom. He was glad the jailhouse was only a short walk away, worried in case some of the farmers present didn't want to wait a week for Bannister's killer to be hanged. If they started trouble the cowboys would be only too glad to finish it.

'I'm sorry, Tom.' Hugh Rowlands, chairman of the Cattlemen's Association, spoke up as the two men reached him. 'If there's anything I can do, just ask.'

'Yeah, thanks, sir.' Rowlands gave a little nod.

Steadman didn't dare look at Amy Mallory as he passed her but he could hear her crying.

Because the courtroom was too small for everyone who'd wanted to attend the trial — the most talked about event in a long while — a crowd had gathered outside. Word of the verdict had gone before Jackson and Steadman. There were some calls of encouragement but they were drowned out by catcalls and boos. Someone threw some old fruit that splattered across Steadman's shoulders.

'Keep back, back!' Jackson yelled, and forced his way through the gathered men and women. He propelled Steadman up on to the sidewalk and in through the open door of his office where Bob Sparks, the jailor, shut it firmly behind him. 'Get through into the cells.'

'I didn't do it,' Steadman repeated.

'Like the judge said you had a fair trial . . . '

'With townspeople and farmers on the jury, oh yeah, very fair!' Steadman said sarcastically. 'Oh, leave me alone, Marshal, go ahead and sort out building the gallows.'

He tried to sound as if he didn't care but left on his own, he sank down on the bunk, head in his hands, his stomach churning. He'd never believed it would come to this.

There hadn't seemed to be much evidence against him and he'd been certain he could trust Mr Rowlands to somehow ensure he was found innocent. He hadn't been worried. Now he saw that was foolish. The judge might not have been against him but the jury certainly were; he hadn't stood a chance. He should have sought help at the beginning, with luck perhaps it wasn't too late to seek help now.

'Marshal, Marshal,' he got up and went over to the cell door.

'What is it?' Jackson asked.

'I want you to send an urgent message over the telegraph for me.'

★   ★   ★

Peter Warren drove the buckboard home from Newberry to his father's farm as fast as he could. It was empty because after he'd heard this latest news he hadn't even stopped to buy the supplies for which he'd gone into town. His father would be annoyed with him but this information was much too important to wait.

Peter was already furious because his father hadn't let him and David go into Newberry for Steadman's trial. He'd longed to see the killer found guilty, especially as he'd been the one to find Bannister's body. He would never forget the shock of riding down to the farm and seeing his hero lying dead and blood-soaked in the yard.

Instead they'd had to wait until one of their luckier neighbours called in with news of the guilty verdict. Now he was even angrier.

As he pulled up before the house, he jumped down almost before the horse had come to a halt. He banged open the door making his parents and two brothers, who were in the kitchen getting ready for the evening meal, jump with fright.

'Pa!' he yelled.

'Whatever is it?' Warren said. 'What's happened?'

Peter paused to get his breath back. 'Guess what? That bastard — '

'Watch your language in front of your mother!'

' — Sorry.' Peter took another deep breath. 'Yesterday, after his trial, Steadman sent a message to that agency he used to work for. The one he's always boasting about.'

'It's some sort of private detective agency, ain't it?' Martin asked.

'Yeah, that's right.'

'Why's he done that?'

'Because, Pa, he's asked for help in proving him innocent of Ralph's murder.'

The others all looked at one another.

'Doesn't that mean he is, in fact, innocent?' Louisa Warren said.

Peter looked at her scornfully. 'Of course it don't, Ma. It just means he's doing everything possible to get out of being hanged. What's more there's been a telegram in reply. A detective is already on his way! Whoever he is he'll be a friend of Steadman's, or in his pay. He'll look at the evidence and turn it around so Steadman is found innocent.'

'I don't see how,' Martin said.

Peter glared at his brother. Why did Martin have to be so reasonable about everything? He was as bad as their mother, always wanting to see both sides. 'The bastard — sorry, Ma — is goin' to get away with it.'

'He can't,' David said, clenching his hands together. 'He shot Ralph; everyone knows that and the jury agreed, he must hang for it.'

'Are you sure about this?' Warren asked.

'Yeah, Pa. It was all over town.'

'And when is this private detective meant to arrive?'

'The day after tomorrow I think. He's coming by train.'

'What are we goin' to do?' That was David, always ready for action.

'There's nothing we can do,' Warren told him with a worried look at Louisa. 'Except trust in the law.'

'Oh, Pa!'

'I don't like this any more than any of you. I had no great liking for Bannister but it certainly seems wrong that his killer might get off because he has connections. But I don't want you boys trying to take the law into your own hands. Do you understand?'

'Yeah, Pa.'

3

Neil Travis glanced across at Zachary Cobb. For the last hour or so the man hadn't spoken or moved but simply sat and stared out of the train window. Not that there was a great deal to see — just a vast and empty valley ringed by the faint purple smudges of far off foothills.

Now Neil ventured, 'Shouldn't be far.'

Cobb just shook his head.

Neil sighed. After he had been knifed and almost killed when helping Cobb go up against a gang of robbers[1] Cobb had treated him carefully, actually been nice to him. That had lasted just as long as it took for Neil to be up and around. Now Cobb was in one of his bad moods, made even worse by the facts that he had recently turned thirty and

---

[1] See *Incident at Wheeler's Canyon*

that he didn't like travelling by train.

Even worse there were only four days to go before Tom Steadman was due to be hanged. Cobb didn't have much time in which to prove him innocent and he never liked the thought of failing.

But, Neil thought, none of that was his fault.

Perhaps Cobb thought the same because pulling out his pocket watch and looking at the time he said, 'About another forty minutes. Once we get to the stop we'll have to hire a couple of horses to complete the journey to Newberry.'

'How long will that take?'

Cobb shrugged. 'I'm not sure. Two hours maybe. We'll be there before nightfall anyway. Thank God.' Once there he could actually sleep in a decent bed.

Cobb was employed by Bellington's Private Detective Agency. As a detective he went where he was sent but sometimes he wished Mr Bellington wouldn't send him to places involving such long and uncomfortable journeys.

Even so Cobb liked, and was good at, his job and didn't want to do anything to jeopardize it. Because Mr Bellington liked his men to look tidy and dress neatly, his dark-brown hair was cut short and he was clean-shaven. He wore sombre suits and white shirts and kept his boots polished.

As well as not allowing his employees to object to what they did and where they went, Mr Bellington had a number of rules for them to obey. While Cobb tried not to break any of them he had broken the one that said the detectives should not, under any circumstances, knowingly consort with outlaws. Neil Travis couldn't exactly be called an outlaw but he had once been a petty thief. And while he couldn't be called a thief any longer either, Mr Bellington would probably not appreciate the distinction and would, if he ever found out, disapprove to say the least.

Cobb still couldn't quite understand

why he'd made the offer to Neil that he should accompany him on his detective work. The young man's dress and looks certainly weren't up to standard, with his long brown hair, wispy moustache and untidy clothes. But since Neil had nearly died in a fight with the Kelman gang, Cobb knew he was used to his company and, even worse, actually liked him. Not that he'd admit that to anyone and certainly never to Neil.

'Did you know this Tom Steadman?' Neil asked, after peering out of the window again.

'Only slightly. He left soon after I joined the agency. He'd got fed up with travelling around the country all the time and wanted to put down roots. But from what I heard he was a skilled detective. And well liked.'

'So you don't believe he killed this homesteader?'

'It does sound surprising but then, as I say, I didn't know him at all well and in, what, six or seven years a man can change. Become someone else to who he once was. After he left the agency I never learned what became of him.' Cobb paused. 'The important thing is Mr Bellington believes he's innocent.'

And wanted it proved. And the hanging stopped.

'It's a pity Steadman didn't contact Mr Bellington earlier. I could have reached Newberry before the trial. Heard the evidence for myself.' As it was, the man had waited until he was found guilty and sentenced to death. Almost three days had been wasted since receiving Steadman's plea for help in making arrangements to come to Newberry and actually travelling to the town.

'Maybe he thought he'd be found innocent,' Neil suggested. 'And perhaps as he's now asked for help that does mean he is innocent.'

Cobb hoped so. Mr Bellington believed he knew people and what they were capable of and he wouldn't be at all pleased to know he was wrong and that Steadman was, in fact, guilty of murder.

'If he didn't shoot Bannister some-one did.'

Cobb didn't say anything about that being obvious.

'So you might find something to show who that was.'

'I hope so.' Prove someone else guilty would prove Steadman innocent.

'I wonder if he had a fair trial.' Neil didn't have much faith in the law or judges.

'That is something else I'll have to try to discover. It was held before a Judge Bowyer. I can't say I know anything about him, good or bad. Ah, looks like we're slowing down.'

Neil stood up, reaching for their bags stowed in the overhead rack.

Before long some ramshackle build-ings came into view. By the railroad tracks was a water-tower, a platform and a tiny office. That was all. Otherwise, the halt was slap bang in the middle of nowhere. With a wail of its whistle the train came to a shuddering stop.

For such a small place it was surprising for Cobb and Neil to find they weren't the only passengers getting off while several people waited to get on.

They stepped down off the platform onto a narrow, dusty road running between a couple of saloons and a tent offering card games. Then came some empty lots before the last building which was a barn with a corral by it, in which were several horses.

Neil rather hoped they could go into one of the saloons for a drink and, more importantly, something to eat. It seemed a long time since they'd eaten at the last train halt. But Cobb was in a hurry to reach Newberry and he walked towards the barn without pausing. It looked to Neil like it was going to be a long time before they ate again.

In front of the barn two horses were tied to the hitching rail. They were sweating as if they had been ridden hard and quite a distance, but there was no sign of their riders, nor of anyone else. Cobb pushed open the door and he and Neil stepped out of the glare of the sunlight into the barn's coolness. It was divided into six stalls, three on either side of a large open area, and was full of the smell of hay and horses.

'Hallo,' Cobb called. 'Anybody here?'

The only answer was a shot! A bullet whizzed by Cobb's ear and embedded itself in a bale of hay.

'Look out!'

Cobb acted swiftly and instinctively. He gave Neil a violent shove that sent him sprawling towards the nearest stall. At the same time he dropped to the floor and squirmed towards the safety of the opposite stall. He was chased all the way by more shots, which kicked up little puffs of dust at his heels. Reaching the partition wall, he glanced across at Neil, thankful to see he was unhurt, and quickly took stock of the situation. The shots were coming from the back of the barn and there were two attackers, probably the riders of the horses out front.

He pulled out his gun and fired back, although he couldn't see a target. More bullets kept him pinned down. This could go on forever. Looking across he saw Neil on his knees also prepared to fire if he could find someone to shoot at. Cobb signalled him to stay where he was, pointing at himself and at the barn door. Neil nodded to show he understood.

Taking a deep breath Cobb jumped up and raced for the door. At the same time Neil fired fast and wildly, hoping to keep their assailants occupied. Cobb reached the door, leapt through it and slammed it shut behind him, feeling it shake as it was struck by several bullets. Without stopping he raced round the side of the barn, jumped the rail of the corral and flattened himself against the barn wall. The horses shifted about nervously but they took no notice of him. Listening to the shooting which was still going on, he inched his way along the wall until he reached the rear door. By his reckoning the two men should be somewhere close by on its other side.

Slowly and carefully he pushed the door open with the barrel of his gun. No shots greeted him. Hopefully the men didn't realize what he was doing, perhaps they thought he had run away.

He peered inside. Yes, there they were! Still occupied. Not quite sure of what was going on. Looking at one another. Looking towards where Neil was. But not thinking to look behind them.

'Hold it right there!' Cobb yelled.

With cries of shock the men stopped firing and glanced round.

'Get to your feet and throw down your guns.'

For a moment it seemed as if the men would do as they were told. Then the one nearest Cobb flung himself sideways and raised his gun. Before he could fire, Cobb shot first. Cobb's bullet struck his assailant full in the face. With a strangled scream the man grabbed at the wound even as he fell on his back. He kicked his legs once or twice and was quiet. Cobb turned from him. The second man was bringing his gun up.

'Don't be stupid.'

It did no good. The man fired once, twice. He was scared, Cobb could see the fear in his eyes, the way his hand and arm shook. The bullets missed.

But the next one might not and Cobb was left with no choice. He took steady aim and pulled the trigger. In a spray of blood the man collapsed behind the hay bale he'd been sheltering against. He groaned once, that was all.

Still holding his gun, Cobb entered the barn and looked down at the men. Both were dead. Neil joined him.

'Wonder who they were,' he said.

'And what they wanted.' Cobb was annoyed he'd had to shoot them before getting the answers to both questions.

Just then several men shoved their way through the barn doors.

'What's goin' on here?' one of them

asked, as he pushed his way to the front and stared down at the two corpses.

'I might ask you the same.' Cobb holstered his gun. 'We came in here and these two men started shooting at us. Anyone recognize them?'

'No.'

'Who owns the barn?'

'I do.' It was the man at the forefront of the crowd.

'What about the horses out front?'

'Never seen 'em before either,' the man said with a couldn't-care-less shrug.

'Did these men want to hire more horses?'

'Nope, at least I dunno. I wasn't here when they arrived.'

'Where were you?'

'Down at the saloon. Can't be here all the time. I guess they must've been thieves and when they spotted you and your companion they thought you'd be easy to rob.'

'These things happen sometimes,' another man said. ''Specially in an out-of-the-way place like this where we ain't got no law.'

'Seems like they was wrong,' someone else said, with a chuckle.

Cobb knew he was unlikely to get any answers here. And, of course, these men might be right.

'I've got somewhere to go,' he said. And he was anxious to be on his way. He didn't want to waste any more time. Every minute would count if he was to prove Steadman innocent. 'Can I leave it to you to bury these two?'

'Yeah, OK.'

'And I need to hire two of your best horses.'

'OK.'

As the crowd drifted away now the excitement was over, Cobb caught hold of Neil's arm.

'I want you to stay here. Find out if anyone knows who these men were and where they came from.'

Neil looked down at the two dead men. 'You don't think they were just out to rob us then?'

'That'd be the simple answer.'

Neil knew Cobb was sometimes suspicious of simple answers.

'But their horses sure had been ridden hard as if the men were in a hurry.'

'But how would anyone have known we were coming here? Or when we'd arrive?'

Cobb shrugged. 'I don't know. Just see what you can learn. Then come on to Newberry, all right?'

'Yeah, sure.'

4

It was late afternoon when the outskirts of Newberry came into view. The trail from the railroad halt led in more or less a straight line across the valley, climbing all the while towards the foothills. Soon Cobb found himself in ranch country, herds of cattle grazing on the sparse grass, a line of sycamore trees in the distance indicating the presence of a stream. It was hot, the sun shining out of a cloudless sky, with barely the hint of a breeze

As he rode through a busy business district it soon became obvious that Newberry was a reasonably prosperous town. Several stores, a bank, a hotel and the marshal's office and small court-house were situated around a well-kept plaza. Down side streets were a couple of boarding-houses, a school and a church. The buildings were made of adobe and overhangs provided welcome shade. Further work was going on here and there. Plenty of people were about and horses and buckboards crowded the dusty roads.

Although Cobb was tired and hungry he decided to visit Marshal Jackson before he did anything else. He was anxious to find out exactly what had happened and what evidence Jackson had discovered to make him arrest Steadman.

The marshal's office appeared to be fairly new. It had a yard at one side out of view of the cells. It was here that a gallows was already being built: out of sight but not out of the hearing of the prisoner.

Cobb dismounted, tied his horse to the hitching rail and went into the cool jailhouse. A young man was sitting at one of the two desks. Another older man, in his sixties, with grey hair and a grey beard and wrinkles round his eyes and mouth sat at the other.

The young man looked up and said, 'Help you?'

'Marshal Jackson?'

'Yeah.'

'I'm Zachary Cobb from Bellington's.'

'Oh yeah. I got the message you were on your way. Owen Jackson.' He stood up to shake Cobb's hand. He was about twenty-eight, of middle height with bushy brown hair and blue eyes. Both his clothes and his gun were well-worn. 'This is Bob Sparks, my jailer.'

Cobb nodded at the old man. Jackson also nodded at him and Sparks hitched up his trousers and left the jailhouse to allow the two lawmen to have their conversation in private.

'Pull up a chair, sit down. Would you like some coffee? It's freshly brewed.'

'Please.'

After Jackson had poured out two mugs of coffee, he sat in his chair and leant forward on his arms. He said, 'Look, let's get it straight from the start: I ain't got any problem with you coming here trying to prove Steadman innocent; I'll give you any help I can, but let me also say straight off I think he's guilty and he was convicted after a fair trial. The evidence convinced Judge Bowyer and a jury.'

'Fair enough.' Cobb would do his job whatever the circumstances, but it always helped if the local law had no objection to his presence. He drank some of the coffee, which was hot and very strong. 'Perhaps you would start by telling me the background to the situation?'

'Sure.' Jackson paused to gather his thoughts then went on, 'This is cattle country, mostly open range. You probably noticed that on your ride up here.'

Cobb nodded.

'There are a number of large ranches roundabout most of which were started soon after the Civil War ended. They've always done well. Lately, over the past five or six years, farmers, homesteaders I mean, have been taking advantage of the offer of title to a hundred and sixty acres to move in.'

'And the ranchers don't like that?'

Cobb knew that ranchers often resented the intrusion on to their lands of farmers and their fences. Believed that as it had always been open range that's the way it should stay.

'No, not particularly,' Jackson said in agreement. 'In fact, it was the coming of the homesteaders that decided the ranchers to set up a Cattlemen's Association. It doesn't just exist to protect the ranchers' interests against the farmers but that's its main aim.'

'And Tom Steadman was employed as a detective?'

'Almost from the start. He was known to one or two of the ranchers as a good man with a gun, and his reputation was helped by him coming from Bellington's. He seemed a sensible choice and for most of the time he's done a good, fair job. Oh, some of the farmers objected to his methods but they had no real complaint. He went up against known rustlers and mostly left the rest alone.' Jackson paused for a moment. 'Given the circumstances, both groups rubbed along fairly well. It's only recently that there've been complaints about Steadman's behaviour, that he's been using unnecessary violence, as well as accusations about ordinary farmers rustling cattlemen's stock.'

'When did all this start'?'

'I'm not sure. It just seemed that a lot of small things suddenly added up to real big trouble.'

'But why? Something must have happened to change things.'

'I know,' Jackson agreed with a little frown. 'But there ain't anything I can put my finger on. Things certainly ain't been helped by a couple of bad seasons. It's always dry down here near the desert as we are, but we've had hardly any rain for well over a year. Things are getting desperate. For everybody. There's jealously and anger where a farmer has fenced off water that a rancher believes was, in the days of the free range, once his own and should still be free to everyone who needs it.

And anger too from the farmers when they believe the ranchers ain't taking any notice of their ownership of the land. Each side thinks it has right on its side.'

'And now the cattlemen are accusing the farmers of wholesale rustling.'

'Yeah.'

'With any justification? Is there any truth to all these accusations?'

'There are faults on both sides.' Jackson raised his hands. 'The farmers ain't perfect and some are surely not above rustling for profit as opposed to taking a cow to feed their family. But the ranchers are making too much of a situation that once they might not have taken any notice of at all.'

'And had Steadman become too violent in trying to uphold the ranchers' interests?'

Jackson shrugged. 'I guess so.'

It was a scene set for trouble. Range wars had started over much less.

'What about the man who killed?'

'Ralph Bannister.' Jackson sighed and stood up to refill their coffee mugs. 'He was part of the trouble. He was a real hot head, always going around saying how the farmers were as good as the ranchers. Said the farmers had as much right to the land as anybody else. And, of course, so they do. It was the way he kept goin' on about it, all of the time. I warned him more'n once that he was making a bad situation worse. Things were hardly helped because his farm included a waterhole that so far has showed no sign of drying up and which he refused to let any of his neighbours use. But he wouldn't listen. He was trying to get the farmers to stand together against the ranchers.'

'Was he succeeding?'

'Partly. Especially amongst the younger ones. One or two of the older farmers tried to keep a lid on the situation but they were beginning to fail. I tell you, Mr Cobb, I didn't like it, I could foresee a helluva fight coming our way, but I'm the town marshal not the county sheriff and there wasn't much I could do except try to keep the two sides separate.'

'But you didn't succeed because Bannister was shot and killed. Or did that solve some of your problems?'

Jackson frowned and said angrily, 'I certainly wasn't happy about it.'

'All right, I'm sorry.' Cobb didn't want to annoy Jackson unnecessarily. And from first impressions he appeared a good man, not one to condone murder, even one that might help him keep the peace, or one to railroad an innocent man because it was convenient. 'Was Steadman your first suspect?'

'About my only one as it turned out, yeah.'

Cobb sat forward. Now they were coming to it. 'Why? What evidence was there?'

'For a start, with Bannister dead, it was going to be easier for Steadman to make sure the rest of the farmers toed the line.'

'But that can't be all?'

'No, of course not.' Jackson sounded angry again as if he suspected Cobb of thinking he hadn't done his job properly. 'Steadman was seen in the area of Bannister's home at the right time.'

'Who by?'

'A couple of hands who work for the Double D ranch. Ben Lucan and Adam Carter. They testified at the trial. Not that they made very good witnesses. Their rowdy and rather stupid behaviour certainly didn't impress the judge. Even so they stuck to what they said. And why should they lie?'

Cobb could think of a number of reasons, the principal one being that they'd been paid to do so. He made a mental note of the names, thinking he would need to speak to them.

'The Double D, where's that?'

'Next to Bannister's farm.'

'Bit of a lucky coincidence.'

'Maybe, but then as Lucan and Carter explained, they happened to be working on the fence that divides the

two properties when they saw Steadman.'

'Anything else?'

'Yeah, Steadman and Bannister were
both courting the same girl.'

'A prostitute?'

Jackson shook his head. 'No, a decent
young woman actually. Amy Mallory.
Her brother owns the livery stable and
Amy helps him.' He shrugged. 'It
wouldn't be the first time that one man
shot another over a girl.'

'Is that it?'

'It's enough.'

It didn't seem much to Cobb but he
knew men had been hanged on even
flimsier evidence.

'Can I see Steadman?'

'Yeah,' Jackson stood up, reaching
into his desk drawer for a bunch of
keys. 'Leave your gun out here and any
other weapons you're carrying.'

Cobb made no objection.

'By the way, Owen, who's the head of
the Cattlemen's Association?'

'A Hugh Rowlands. He owns the

Flying R, which is the area's most important and largest ranch. It's lands stretch almost down to the Mexican border. He's a good man. He didn't like the way things seemed to be spiralling out of control any more'n I did.'

'Are you sure about that?'

'Yeah, I am. And he'll be willing to talk to you because neither does he like the idea of his employee being hung for a murder he says he didn't commit.' Jackson unlocked the door at the rear of the office. 'OK, Mr Cobb, it's through here. Take as long as you like.'

5

There were four cells, two on either side of a short passage. Each had a barred window high up on the wall, two bunks and a chair. Only one cell was occupied.

As Cobb went up to the bars, Tom Steadman rose from the bunk where he'd been lying, staring up at the ceiling, and came over to him. Although it had been some time since Steadman left the detective agency, Cobb recognized him immediately. The man was now forty. He was almost as tall as Cobb's six feet, and barrel chested, with fair hair balding in the front. He had a drooping moustache. Even in jail he was dressed well and, despite the fact he was waiting to be hanged, he had a cocky look about him which Cobb thought wouldn't go down well with a lot of people.

'Zac, you're here at last!'

'Journey took nearly three days,' Cobb said, not happy at having to justify himself.

'A goddamn long three days since the judge said I was to hang and I've been stuck in here with nothing to do but wait for the gallows to be built. It is being built, ain't it? I can hear 'em sawing and hammering the wood.'

'You should have gotten in touch before.'

Steadman smiled to show he'd meant no offence. 'Didn't think I'd ever come to this sorry pass.' He spoke lightly but his hands gripped the bars so tightly his knuckles turned white. With an effort he relaxed and smiled again.

'Well I'm here now. And from what Jackson has told me it don't seem like he had much of a case against you.'

'It was enough to convince judge and jury. But then the jury was made up of townsfolk and homesteaders, my natural enemies, with nary a rancher or cowhand amongst 'em, so I guess they weren't that hard to convince. Most've been looking for an excuse to do me down.'

'Any reason for that? Apart from the fact that you work for the Cattlemen's Association.'

Steadman shrugged. 'That was enough to make me unpopular with most. You know how it is!' He paused then said, 'I suppose I'd best admit there've been times when I've had to be harsh with some of the homesteaders, especially recently since they've insisted on rustling cattle. At my trial it was said I'd been terrorizing 'em. Now that, Zac, is an unkind word. And untrue. I've never done anything to anyone who didn't deserve it.'

At least according to the wishes of the ranchers, Cobb thought. What the farmers felt about it was probably something quite different.

'Tom, I've got to ask, did you shoot and kill this Ralph Bannister?'

'Absolutely not. No way.' Steadman shook his head. 'I ain't about to say I ain't never shot no one, because I have, both during my time with Mr Bellington and since coming here to work for the ranchers. But it was always a case of shoot or be shot and I always gave the other man a fighting chance. I expect it's the same with you.'

'But Bannister was causing trouble wasn't he? Was trying to get the farmers to band together?'

'True. He was a godawful pain in the ass. And his death meant the farmers quietened down. For a while anyway. But once they started to get over their fear of being shot it only made 'em more mean and determined.'

Cobb nodded. That was a good point.

'If I'd gone up against him I'd've had a better reason than the fact he was stirring up trouble. Christ, if that was a good enough reason to call someone out I'd've been damn busy. And I would've done it face to face. I would never ever dry-gulch anyone.'

Cobb believed him and not just because he wanted to. He felt that for

Steadman to kill someone from ambush would be to take something away from his prowess as a shooter and as a man. He would prefer other people to know he was so good with a gun he wasn't scared to play by the rules. He was sure Neil would say that was a bit like Cobb himself.

'Any idea who did?'

'No,' Steadman said, with another shake of his head. 'Bannister wasn't all that popular, especially with the ranchers, but not with some of the farmers either, he was too quick to anger for that, too quick with his fists, but I don't know of anyone he'd annoyed enough or anything he'd done to be killed for.' He shrugged, then went on, 'It's a long shot but you might take a look at Fred Warren.'

'Who's he?'

'A farmer. He's been here for a long time, I think he was one of the first to take up title to land along the creek, and he's gotten himself a decent place which he's always trying to improve.

Until Bannister began to stir things up, Warren was the unofficial leader of the farmers but at the same time he was always reasonable enough.'

'Why would he shoot Bannister? Another farmer.'

'To be honest I wouldn't suspect him at all except that two of his three sons were under Bannister's influence and were eager to join him in whatever he was doing. Had taken to wearing guns, were likely to be in the forefront of any fighting. I know it ain't likely but Warren could've decided to shoot Bannister rather than risk his sons being hurt.'

He didn't sound very hopeful.

'What about the cattlemen?'

'What about 'em?'

'Could one of them have decided you'd become too violent and wanted to be rid of you? And so they killed Bannister and put the blame on you. In other words killed two annoying birds with one stone.'

'What, betrayed me?' Steadman gave

a snort of derision. 'Not likely.'

'It wouldn't be the first time.'

'That'd mean a rancher had to kill Bannister.'

'And you don't see that happening?'

'Oh yeah, only too easily, someone had to after all. But not then to put the blame on me, no. Why should anyone do that? I worked for the cattlemen, have done so for a long while, and I did a good job too. Never had any complaints anyway. And if they wanted to be rid of me all they'd have to do is fire me.'

'You don't know of any reason one of them might have had to want you dead?'

Steadman thought about that. 'I daresay I've got on the wrong side of one or two of 'em in my time but not enough for murder.' He laughed. 'Seems to me like you're clutching at straws, old son.'

Cobb frowned. He knew Steadman was right but he didn't like the man pointing it out to him. And, as he himself said, someone had to have killed Bannister and maybe there was some motive behind it that they hadn't as yet learned.

'Zac, listen, forget about the association. The ranchers have always treated me right. Treated me like an equal. Mr Rowlands paid for my defence. They'll support me all the way.'

'Right up to the time you're hanged?'

'The law found me guilty; the ranchers can't break the law for me.'

Cobb didn't say anything to that piece of moonshine. He thought Steadman was foolish to be convinced that the ranchers were his friends and would never do him harm, but there didn't seem any point in saying so. Instead he turned back to the evidence against the man.

'What about the fact that two cowhands saw you hanging around Bannister's farm the day of the shooting? What were you doing there?'

'It was a lie. Or they were mistaken. I was never out by Bannister's farm. Not that day anyway.'

'Where were you?'

'Riding around, keeping a look-out for rustlers, but not there.'

'Can you prove that?'

''Course not, or I would've done so.'

Cobb hid a sigh. Proving Steadman innocent wasn't going to be easy, especially as Steadman himself wasn't exactly being co-operative.

'Then there's the rumour that your young lady, Amy Mallory, was also being courted by Bannister.'

Steadman let go of the bars and paced the cell for a moment or two before coming back to Cobb. His eyes blazed. 'That was a lie too.'

'But you'd heard the rumours?'

'Yeah. And I was angry about 'em.' It would have been useless for Steadman to deny that, for anger still showed in his every movement. 'For Amy's sake. I love Amy. Before all this happened I wanted to marry her and settle down. But I didn't go off half cock and shoot Bannister. Instead I asked Amy if there was any truth in the rumours. She said no. I believed her.'

'Who started the rumours?'

'I don't know. I wish I did.' Steadman grinned again. 'None of this is very helpful is it?'

'Not really.'

'I guess you're going to have your work cut out finding enough evidence to set me free, especially as you ain't got much time!'

'I'll do my best.'

'I surely do hope so!'

6

Reggie Drake downed his third whiskey in one long swallow, put the glass down on the bar and belched loudly.

'Fill 'er up!'

Ed Chadwin was torn between doing what Reggie wanted, especially as when Reggie was in town he was one of his best customers, and getting rid of the rancher before he became drunk. He could see a couple of younger towns-men over in one corner laughing at Reggie's antics. If Reggie also spotted them there would be hell to pay. The last thing he wanted in his saloon was a shooting.

'Thought you was meant to be in town to buy supplies.'

Reggie frowned as if trying to remember. 'Oh, yeah,' he said at last. 'Al wants some things. I've got a list here somewhere.' He patted his shirt pockets and pulled out a piece of paper, peering at it.

'Then hadn't you better go and order 'em?'

'But I want another drink.'

'Plenty of time for that later on. As well as a visit to Madam Josephine's. Heard tell she's got a new gal in, just off the Eastern stage.' Chadwin winked. 'Also heard she ain't never had a man before and is waiting for the right one to come along and teach her what to do.' And if you believed that, he thought, then you must've come off the same stage!

But Reggie, being Reggie, was of the opinion that he was extremely good-looking and so wonderful at making love that the girls employed at Madam Josephine's brothel loved him for himself and not because they were paid to do so.

'Really?' he said dreamily. 'Is she pretty?'

'Ain't all of Madam Josephine's girls?'

Reggie's mind was soon made up.

He'd buy what was needed and then take himself off to the brothel. Allan was waiting back at the ranch, not just for the supplies but more importantly the latest news. But Reggie, with three whiskies inside him fuelling his bravado, didn't intend to go home until he was good and ready. His oft-repeated excuse for his behaviour was that as he worked hard he deserved to play hard as well.

He stumbled out on to the street and walked in an unsteady gait towards the plaza. As he got there the door to the marshal's office opened and a stranger came out; a well-armed stranger.

Quickly Reggie took a step back into the shadows cast by the general store, not wanting to be seen. Was this the private detective meant to be coming to help Tom Steadman? How could it be? But if not, then who was he? For a moment his hand toyed with his gun, but even he wasn't foolish enough to backshoot a man in broad daylight in the middle of the town. He watched as the man went to the horse tied to the hitching rail and began to lead it towards the business district.

Reggie searched in his befuddled mind for the answers to the questions about the man's identity Allan would ask. Perhaps as the stranger was heading for the livery he could ask Amy Mallory about him. His brother probably wouldn't like that but then Allan wasn't here to stop him.

*   *   *

As Cobb had to stable his horse he decided to talk to Amy Mallory at the same time, find out how she felt about Steadman; and Bannister.

The livery stable stood at the far end of town, next to the feed and grain store. There was a large corral out back where a man with brown leathery skin was forking hay into a trough. A woman carrying a saddle and bridle came out of the stables. Her brown curly hair was pinned back from her face and she was dressed in a man's shirt and a divided skirt.

'Miss Mallory?' Cobb said, coming to a halt by the rail.

Both the woman and man stopped what they were doing and looked round.

'Yes?' The answer was both an affirmation of her identity and a question as to why she was being asked.

'I'm Zachary Cobb. From the Bellington's Detective Agency. I'd like to talk to you about Tom Steadman.'

'Oh, yes.' She smiled slightly. 'Tom said you were coming. That he knew you from the old days. I'm Amy Mallory. This is my brother, Greg. Why don't you leave your horse in the corral and come inside where it's cooler.'

As he followed the Mallorys into the stable, Cobb saw that Amy was about twenty-nine. She was quite tall and rail thin and while she wasn't particularly pretty her face had character. And determination. He could understand why Tom Steadman had fallen in love with her.

'Are you going to be able to help Tom?' she asked, and up close Cobb could also see a sad expression on her face.

'I hope so.'

'Me and Greg will do whatever we can to help, won't we, Greg?'

Her brother, who was slightly older than Amy and obviously a man of few words, nodded in agreement.

'I'm sure, no, I know, Tom's innocent. He would never, ever shoot anyone from ambush.'

'I don't think he would either.' Cobb paused. 'Miss Mallory, Tom tells me that he's in love with you. Are you in love with him?'

Amy reddened and Greg looked at Cobb angrily.

'I'm sorry to ask such a personal question but it's important I find out the truth.'

'Yes, of course. It's OK, Greg, I don't mind. Yes, Mr Cobb, I love Tom. Very much. He asked me to marry him before all this trouble started. And I said yes.' It was obvious she was telling the truth.

'Then what do you say about the rumours that Ralph Bannister was also courting you?'

This time Greg Mallory took a step forward, hands bunching into fists at his sides. Amy put out a hand to stop him.

'Were the rumours true?'

'No, they most certainly were not! And that's what I told Tom. Who believed me. I hardly knew Bannister. Oh, I admit I spoke to him if I saw him when he came to town to buy supplies, especially if he was staying overnight and left his horse and buckboard here. That was all. I couldn't understand it when I learned what people were saying about me and him.'

'Did he ever mention liking you?'

'No,' Amy said again. 'Our conversations concerned things like the weather or the price of hay. Just like the conversations I have with countless other men. He was always polite, never anything more.'

'Did he speak to you about Steadman?'

'Why should he?'

'Well, he probably knew you two were courting . . . '

'It certainly wasn't a secret.'

' . . . So perhaps if he did have some feelings for you he might not have approved because he was a farmer and Steadman was working for the ranchers.'

'Apart from the fact it was nothing whatsoever to do with him I really can't remember him even once talking to me about personal matters!' Amy was most indignant. 'And if he had, as you say, felt something for me he would have said so. Bannister wasn't the type to keep quiet.'

'That he weren't.' Greg Mallory spoke for the first time.

Amy shook her head, looking upset and almost tearful. 'I don't know who put around such a lie about me or why.'

Cobb said, 'The why might be easy. I doubt it was anything to do with you personally. But it gave Steadman another reason to kill Bannister. Or at least another excuse for people to believe he did.'

'Yes, that's quite likely.' Amy thought about that for a moment or two then burst out, 'Oh, Mr Cobb, I can't tell you how angry and distressed I am at being used in such a way to hurt Tom. It's simply not fair.'

Greg put his arm around his sister and scowled at Cobb as if this was his fault.

'Is there anything else you can tell me that might help?'

Twisting her hands together, Amy shook her head. 'Marshal Jackson already came round asking the same thing, didn't he, Greg? But there was nothing we could tell him. I wish there was.'

'Look, Miss Mallory, there's not much time till the hanging. I can only do so much. Can you and your brother ask around town, try to find out who started the rumours? That could be important.' It would also give Amy something to do, keep her mind occupied.

'Yes, all right. What are you going to do next?'

'I thought I'd visit Mr Rowlands. Discover what the Cattlemen's Association thinks about all this.'

'His place is easy to reach,' Amy said. She went to the door of the stables and pointed. 'Follow the trail out of town towards the foothills and when you come to a fork in the road, take the left-hand one. It'll take you a couple of hours to reach the house.'

'OK, thanks.'

Amy held out her hand for Cobb to shake. 'Good luck, Mr Cobb, I'll be praying you succeed.'

* * *

Although the marshal said people were already starting to arrive for the hanging, Cobb managed to get two rooms in Mrs Penrose's boarding house, which Jackson had recommended as clean and cheap. He was pleased because Mr

Bellington didn't like his detectives to spend more money than was necessary and he didn't want to share with Neil, who snored. His room was on the first floor and the other much cheaper one was in the attics. For a few cents more Mrs Penrose offered breakfast and an evening meal.

That evening Cobb sat alone at a small table under the window of the pleasant dining-room, eating beef stew with potatoes and onions followed by a huge portion of apple pie. There were several other guests: a couple of ranchers and their wives and two drummers who sat together and discussed stage-coach timetables and the difficulty of travelling in the West.

After Mrs Penrose brought him over a mug of steaming coffee, he sat back in his chair and thought over the little he'd learned.

He had already made up his mind that Steadman was innocent. The evidence against him wasn't up to much. No one had actually seen him

65

pull the trigger. And anyone, for whatever reason, could have killed Bannister and put the blame on Steadman, knowing it would be easy to do so. More importantly Steadman's character was such it seemed impossible to imagine him shooting someone from ambush.

But, of course, unless he found some evidence, what he believed wouldn't convince the judge to reopen the case.

He liked Amy. She was genuine and genuinely in love with Steadman. But what was behind the rumour about her and Bannister?

As well as visiting Hugh Rowlands he hoped to find the time to talk to a couple of the homesteaders. This Fred Warren for one. Discover what they felt about Steadman and Bannister. And he must speak to the two Double D witnesses.

There was a lot to do and little time in which to do it. He had a bad feeling about this case. He thought he might fail and an innocent man be hanged while the real killer escaped.

And there was the attack on him and Neil. Was that connected to all this or was it, as the barn-owner believed, a robbery gone wrong? Perhaps Neil would be able to find out.

By the time he went to bed, Neil still hadn't put in an appearance. He hoped the young man hadn't got lost but wouldn't be surprised to learn that he had.

7

Watched by a couple of idlers and the curious barn owner, who said his name was Lenny, Neil went through the saddle-bags on the two horses. He wasn't sure what he was looking for or what he would do with it.

'So, son, you say this Cobb fella is some sorta lawman?' Lenny pushed his hat to the back of his head, scratching hard.

'Yeah. He's a private detective. He works for a very famous agency.'

'And you're his assistant?'

'That's right.' Neil was glad Cobb wasn't there to hear him say that, not that he'd have said it if Cobb was nearby.

'So you're a detective too?'

'Yeah' Neil closed his eyes for a moment. Please, God, don't ever let Cobb find out what he'd said!

'And he thinks these two weren't just out to rob you but were actually gunning for you?'

'Mr Cobb don't like coincidences.'

'But, son, how did they know you were coming in on the train?'

Neil didn't know the answer to that, after all he wasn't really a detective, so he didn't reply. He couldn't blame Lenny for being doubtful, it did seem unlikely that their attackers knew about them. But Cobb's instincts were usually right.

There wasn't much in the saddle-bags. No papers to identify who the men were, not that Neil would have been any the wiser if there had been, as he couldn't read or write. No spare clothes. It didn't seem that the men had been travelling on to any place from here. It did begin to look as if they had ridden here for a purpose, which was to kill him and Cobb, and with the deed done they intended to ride back to wherever they came from. But had they done it for themselves or because someone paid them? If the latter then that someone was likely waiting for their report right now and would have a long wait if so!

Neil went up to the horses that Lenny had unsaddled and was in the process of rubbing down. He ran his hand over the brand on each. It was the same.

'D'you know what this brand is and who owns it?'

Lenny scratched his head again. 'Let's looksee. Two Ds. Double D. No, don't mean nothing to me.'

One of the idlers came closer and stared hard at the brand. 'Hell,' he said, some excitement in his voice. 'Yeah. There's a Double D ranch over near Newberry.'

Newberry! Where Cobb and Neil were going.

'D'you know who it belongs to?'

'Yeah, to a couple of brothers. They've only been there for a few months, what's their name? Um, let's see, yeah, Drake, that's right.'

'Are you sure?' Lenny asked.

'Sure I'm sure.'

'So it's a new ranch?' Neil said.

'Not really, son. It used to be owned by a family from back East but they sold up and went away when the wife got took sick. It was empty for a while, then these two brothers bought it. Heard tell they were boasting about how they were goin' to make a real go of it and become rich and famous.'

'Those men Mr Cobb shot weren't the Drake brothers were they?'

'Nope.' The man shook his head. 'At least I don't think so. I didn't never see the Drakes but someone said they were young guys. In their mid-twenties.'

'Does the name mean anything to you, son?' Lenny said. He finished with the horses and set them free in the corral.

'No.'

'Well, those two musta worked for 'em, 'lessen of course they stole the horses.'

'I'd better be off. Tell Mr Cobb this.

It might be important.'

'You leave now it'll be dark by the time you get halfway to Newberry,' Lenny warned. 'Why don't you stay here for the night and have a drink and something to eat? Leave first thing in the morning.'

'There's a gal works in the saloon will suit a good-looking lad like you,' the other man added.

Neil was tempted. He gave in to temptation.

'OK,' he said.

★　★　★

It was late when Reggie Drake decided he ought to ride back to the Double D. He'd enjoyed himself with Madam Josephine's new girl and would have liked to stay the night, but Allan would be cross if he did and it was foolish to annoy Allan unnecessarily. He wandered down to the livery stable to collect his horse. He was sorry Amy Mallory wasn't there and decided it would be pointless to ask Greg about the stranger. Greg's conversation usually consisted of grunts and mutters, especially with those he didn't like. And Reggie knew he came well down on the list of Greg's friends. The stable-owner would never answer any questions he didn't want to.

The brothers had purchased their ranch five months before. It was large, spreading up into the foothills, and they both intended it should soon become even bigger. A stream ran through it, although they'd found that after the last couple of years with such little rain this had dried to a mere trickle. The grass was already browning and Allan had decided that the cattle would soon have to be moved up into the foothills.

In good times they could probably run twice as many cows as they had now. But times were bad and things weren't working out quite as they — both ambitious to make money and a mark on the world — hoped and planned.

It was dark and the place quiet when Reggie arrived at the ranch house. The few men they could afford to employ were asleep in the bunkhouse. He left his horse in the corral and walked across the dusty strip of land to the house which he and Allan wanted to enlarge and improve. The light of an oil lamp showed in the parlour window. Allan was still up.

Reggie took a deep breath before going inside. Allan wouldn't like what he had to say.

'Well?' His brother stopped pacing as soon as Reggie closed the door behind him. 'What happened? You've been a long time. I expected you back before this.' Allan sniffed. 'Did you stop off in the saloon? You did, didn't you? How could you? You knew how anxious I was.'

Allan was twenty-seven, the older of the two brothers, Reggie being three years younger. He was also the worrier of the two. Reggie seldom let anything much worry him or for long. Despite their different temperaments it was obvious from their looks that they were brothers. Both had the same cleft chin, brown eyes and dark-brown hair, although Allan's had a bald spot in the middle and Reggie's was long and curly.

Deliberately keeping his brother waiting, Reggie went over to the cupboard and poured himself out a whiskey. He turned, raising the glass. 'Want one?'

'No! What is it? What's wrong?'

'I think the private detective arrived in town.'

'Hell!' Allan sounded as if he couldn't believe it and he clutched at the back of the nearest chair as if his legs wouldn't support him. 'Don't drink so much. You've had enough already. What do you mean *think*? You might be wrong. Didn't you find out for sure?'

'There was a stranger in with Marshal Jackson. I saw him. I guess it was the detective, but I couldn't very well go in and ask who he was, could I?'

'You should have found some way to find out.'

'Well, I didn't.'

'Hell, what are we going to do?' Allan passed a hand over his thinning hair.

'Don't think there's much we can do.'

'We must do something.'

'Don't fret, Al. It'll all be over in a few days. No one'll ever guess all we've done. How can they? They ain't as clever as us.'

Allan sighed. If only life was as simple as Reggie believed. Of course Reggie was right when he said they were cleverer than anyone else around here, but all the same he could think of several things that might go wrong before they were home and clear. Especially as it looked as if something had already gone wrong. It just proved that if you wanted anything done it was best to do it yourself and not rely on others.

'Did you see Miss Mallory? he asked.

'Unfortunately not.' Reggie grinned

and added slyly, 'I expect she was at the jailhouse, holding Steadman's hands through the bars.'

'Shut up!' Allan took a deep breath and clenched his fists by his sides, determined not to let his brother ruffle him. Besides, he told himself, it was only natural Amy would visit Steadman. He also reassured himself it was a situation that couldn't last much longer. Time to change the subject. 'I've been thinking.'

Reggie sighed. That meant more hard work.

'Why don't we move some of our cows on to Bannister's land?'

'What! Do you think so?' Reggie was shocked at the suggestion and for once was the one sounding caution.

'Why not? All the water over there is just going to waste.'

'Supposing someone sees?'

'Who? Everyone's too busy in town waiting for the hanging. And if our cows should be found by the waterhole we can say we know nothing about it and they must have got there by accident. I think it's worth the risk.'

'Perhaps you're right.'

'You know I am.'

'OK, Al, we'll start tomorrow.' Reggie downed his whiskey. 'I'm off to bed. You should go too. Get some sleep. Everything'll turn out all right, trust me.'

Allan watched him go. Then he poured himself out his own drink and drank it quickly.

8

Although it was early when Cobb finished his breakfast and left for the stables, the stores were already opening up and sidewalks being swept clean, while three women gossiped on the corner before starting their shopping. Greg Mallory was at work and he saddled Cobb's horse and managed to say enough to wish him good luck.

Following the directions Amy had given him, it wasn't long before Cobb rode by a tall arch of horns in the middle of the trail, a sign over the top announcing 'The Flying R'. It soon became obvious he was on a prosperous ranch. Bunches of cattle grazed here and there, becoming more numerous the further on he rode. In the distance he glimpsed a couple of cowboys driving more cows up towards the foothills.

About an hour later, a rider topped the slope of a nearby hill and came galloping towards him. As the man got closer Cobb saw he already had his rifle out and held in front of him, ready for action.

Cobb pulled his horse to a halt and waited.

The man proved to be in his early forties, thickset with a handlebar moustache. His working clothes were covered with dust. He stopped a little way away, looking at Cobb with hard and wary eyes.

'You're on private land,' he said. 'All this hereabouts belongs to Mr Rowlands. Didn't you see the sign?'

'It's Mr Rowlands I want to talk to.' Cobb kept his hands clear of the saddlehorn, wanting the other man to know he wasn't about to make any sudden moves.

'Oh, yeah? What about exactly?'

'I'm from Bellington's Detective Agency. Here to help Tom Steadman.'

The man relaxed a little, although he

still kept a tight grip on his rifle.

'Oh yeah, Tom said he'd sent a message to his old employer. OK.' He decided to trust Cobb. 'It's this way. It ain't far now. You're lucky Mr Rowlands is home at the ranch headquarters today. He's expecting to talk to you, although I ain't sure what help he'll be. He don't know anything about the shooting. I'm Sam Porter, Rowlands' foreman, by the way.'

Cobb introduced himself.

'Sorry about the rifle but the way things are none of us can afford to take any chances.'

'I understand.' Cobb never took any chances either. He kicked his horse forward and the two men rode side by side up the slope.

'Did you know Steadman?'

'Yeah, but not well. He had his job to do and I had mine. He mostly dealt with the ranchers not their men.'

Porter sounded as if he didn't approve of Steadman, or his job, and Cobb didn't bother to ask him anything more. It was clear the foreman couldn't, or wouldn't, help either. Instead he changed the subject and said, 'You're running a lot of cattle here.'

'Not as many as in the past. There ain't enough grass left. Damn weather!'

It was only a short while until they were riding down to the ranch head-quarters.

Porter said, 'I'll introduce you to Mr Rowlands and then be about my business.'

Cobb looked round. It appeared to him that, despite the worry over the lack of rain, Hugh Rowlands was doing well.

There were two corrals, surrounded by well-cared for work buildings, a long bunkhouse and a couple of shacks. Several cowhands wandered around, all looking busy. The horses were sleek and well fed. And halfway up a slope shaded by cypress trees was the house itself. It was a handsome building, two storeys high, with large windows and a porch running all the way round.

Hugh Rowlands was a big man, too. He had black hair, greying in places, and dark eyes. He invited Cobb to sit on the porch with him and his wife brought out a tray with glasses and a jug of homemade lemonade. Giving Cobb a shy smile she poured them some before disappearing back inside. Rowlands sat in a rocker, feet up on the rail.

'You've got a nice place here,' Cobb said, nodding at the activity round the corrals.

'That I have,' Rowlands said in self-satisfaction.

'Have you been here long?'

'My wife and I came out to Arizona just after the Civil War ended. I'd fought for the North and could've gone back to my folks' farm in Maine, but I don't know,' he shrugged, 'I felt dissatisfied. I wanted something different, something more challenging, probably to take my mind off the terrible things I'd seen in the fighting. Luckily my wife agreed with me. We decided to settle here as soon as we saw the land. Good land. It was difficult at first what with the Indians and damn outlaws, and I know it can be difficult at times now, but on the whole it's a decent place to bring up a family. Have you got a wife? Children?'

'No.' Cobb shook his head. 'One day maybe.'

'They're both a worry and a pleasure. Wouldn't be without any of 'em.' Rowlands smiled and looked back out at his land. 'Be even better if it'd rain.'

'Everyone seems to mention that.'

'It's only natural. We're all affected. Ranchers and farmers alike. But look at the sky, not even the sign of a damn cloud.' The man paused. 'Still you're not here to listen to our woes. You're here to talk about Tom Steadman.'

'That's right. What do you think, sir? Do you think he's guilty?'

Rowlands frowned. 'A short while ago I'd've said no. But now I'm not so sure. In the same way I would also have said that while I don't like or approve of sodbusters coming out here and fencing off the open range we never had much trouble with 'em in the past.'

'But Marshal Jackson, as well as Steadman seems to think you're having trouble now.'

'Look, Mr Cobb, I don't mind anyone taking the odd cow or two to help feed a starving family. That's understandable. But we can't put up with wholesale rustling. I know some of the farmers are having a hard time but so are we.'

'So a lot of rustling is going on?'

'Yeah, I'm afraid so. My ranch isn't affected, well, my foreman tells me I have lost some cows but not enough to make a difference but others around here are suffering badly.' Rowlands paused to pour more lemonade. 'We ranchers have got to stick up for ourselves and support one another. That's not unreasonable, is it?'

'No. I expect the farmers feel the same.'

Rowlands' eyes narrowed as if he didn't like Cobb taking the opposite point of view.

'Of course out here near to the border with Mexico we've always been plagued by rustlers and enjoyed little in the way of protection from the law. In fact, up until a few years ago Newberry didn't have any law! It's what we employed Steadman for in the first place. And I was in complete agreement when Steadman strung some of the bastards up. Even let my men help him.'

Cobb nodded. He knew that sort of thing often happened, even though he didn't really approve. He would rather the law was upheld but that wasn't always possible.

'He did a good and necessary job for us. Cleared out most of the bastards, except for the foolhardy. But now the rustling is back and, as there are no reports of outlaws coming into the area, it must be the homesteaders who are responsible.'

'What does Jackson have to say about the situation?'

'Mostly that he's town marshal and can't help.' Rowlands sighed. 'That's unfair, because of course, he's right. Sometimes we get a visit from the county sheriff but not very often. Newberry is a long way away from anywhere. He don't like to make the journey 'less he has to.'

'And so you asked Steadman to handle the situation? To take the law into his own hands?'

The rancher frowned, perhaps thinking Cobb was criticising him again. Hands clenching together, he said, 'It was his job to help us. He knew how far to go, or at least I thought he did.'

'And did he capture any more rustlers?'

'There was one family, the Pemberley brothers. Five of the silly bastards. Steadman caught 'em driving some cattle belonging to the Drakes down near the border heading for Mexico. He administered punishment.'

'He hung 'em?'

'No. They were beaten up. And told they would be hanged if they didn't leave the area. They left. He handled it well. That's why his other behaviour is surprising.'

'What other behaviour?' Cobb put his glass of lemonade on the tray.

'Well, I, among others, felt he was becoming too violent. So much so I was thinking of proposing to the members of the Association that he be sacked.' Rowlands' voice died away.

'But if he did no more than beat up the Pemberleys, who were known and admitted rustlers, what had he done to make you think he was becoming too violent?' Cobb was puzzled, it didn't make sense to him.

'Well . . . ' Rowlands came to a halt, as if he was also puzzled. 'I'm not exactly sure. There were stories . . . ' He paused. 'Even so I'm surprised it came to murder.'

'Was there any suspicion that Bannister was a rustler?'

'Not as far as I know.'

'What did you think of him? Did he have any enemies?'

'He was a good farmer and with the land he had he really didn't need to rustle. But he was a hot-head and a troublemaker. He wasn't afraid of anyone and he and Steadman had already had one or two run-ins. I'd heard he annoyed several other people as well. And then, of course, there were the stories about him and Amy Mallory.' Rowlands leant forward. 'You want to talk to Fred Warren. He's a homesteader. A decent guy. Hard-worker. He'll be able to tell you more about Bannister. I know he didn't like him much especially because a couple of his boys were influenced by the man's rabble rousing.'

'Yeah, Tom's already mentioned him. I also want to speak to the two cowhands who claim they saw Steadman out near Bannister's place the day he was shot.'

'Ah yeah.' Rowlands finished his

drink of lemonade. 'Lucan and Carter.'

'What's the matter?' Cobb asked, because something was obviously wrong.

'Let's just say I would never employ men like that on my ranch. They were insolent and always bragging about the notches on their guns. And I'd never consider them the most reliable of witnesses.'

'Jackson said much the same.'

'Even so Tom's lawyer couldn't shake their claims.'

'What about this Double D ranch where they worked? Who owns that?'

'The Drake brothers. Allan and Reggie. In their twenties.' Rowlands wrinkled his nose as if he didn't approve of them any more than he approved of their men. 'They bought the place four or five months ago. Claimed themselves a large spread. And they're always boasting about turning it into the largest and richest ranch around Newberry. And then becoming the best ranchers. Want to build a house bigger than mine. As if it was all the easiest thing in the world! Talk about idiots! Still Allan works hard enough, although Reggie fancies himself a ladies' man and spends as much time in town as he can.'

'What about the rest of the men they employ?'

Rowlands shrugged. 'As far as I know neither brother nor any of their men break the law, except for maybe getting thrown in jail for getting drunk on a Saturday night. Nor can I think of any reason why they should try to make trouble for Steadman.'

That was something Cobb intended to find out. 'Perhaps the fact that Bannister's homestead ran along part of the Drakes' land had something to do with it.'

Rowlands frowned again. 'Hmm, maybe, but the Drakes have got plenty of good land already.'

But, Cobb thought, they wanted more, and according to what he'd learned, Bannister's land was even better.

'Ah good, here's my wife to tell me dinner is ready.' Rowlands looked up at her with a smile. 'Stay, won't you? It'll only take a moment to lay an extra place, won't it dear?'

Mrs Rowlands nodded.

'OK, thanks.'

9

Fred Warren came into the farmhouse after a busy morning digging over a field in which he hoped eventually to grow potatoes, which the citizens of Newberry were always eager to buy. The land was full of rocks and stumps of old trees and he had been at work since early light and had not yet cleared half of the field. His wife, Louisa, stood at the stove, getting the midday meal ready. She had spent most of her morning watering the vegetables that she grew near to the house to cook for the family.

It was hot weather and hot work. As he stepped into the kitchen, Warren took off his hat and wiped the sweat away from his face and neck with his bandanna.

'Dinner's nearly ready,' Louisa said, turning to look at him. 'Wash your hands and I'll serve it up.'

'Where're the boys? I expected them to come out and help me. I could've done with their strength. The work could've been finished if they'd put in an appearance.' He stared at Louisa, who refused to meet his eyes. He knew that look. 'Where are they?' he added harshly.

Louisa replied reluctantly, 'I'm sorry, Fred, they've gone into Newberry.'

'Oh for God's sake!' Warren thumped the table. 'Couldn't you have stopped them?' Which he knew was unfair of him to expect.

Louisa was no better pleased than her husband at their sons' behaviour. But she tried not to show it because she knew Fred had a hot temper and tended to treat them as if they were still youngsters rather than grown men.

She sometimes feared he would drive them away. Feared that Peter, the eldest at twenty-one, would leave to begin his own farm rather than wait and take over this one, on which Fred had put in so much time and effort. David, at seventeen, didn't want to become a farmer anyway, as he wasn't fond of the early mornings and long days involved. She had far fewer worries about Martin, the middle boy, the one who took after his father.

He'd ridden away with the other two not because he wanted to go, he knew his father needed help and would rather have been working with him, but only because she'd asked him to keep an eye on his brothers, not let them do anything silly. Although once Peter, and especially David, got an idea in their heads she doubted whether Martin would be able to stop them acting on it.

'What've they gone there for?' Warren demanded. 'It's because of all this trouble, ain't it?'

Louisa nodded and sighed. 'They're still angry. Not only over Bannister's shooting but over the way the farmers are still being molested. They and some of the other younger ones are meeting up to discuss the situation. Oh, Fred, I did try to stop them but they wouldn't listen to me.'

'I'll have their hides,' Warren said, clenching his hands into fists. 'Not only because they're acting stupidly, but worse, they've caused you upset.'

Louisa went up to him and put her arms round him. 'Fred, don't. It won't do any good. Please. I'm just so worried they'll get into trouble.'

Or worse, with the way all three of them were wearing guns.

'Don't fret, Louisa,' Warren comforted her. 'Worrying won't do any good.'

'I know but I can't help it.' With a heavy heart, she turned back to the stove to begin serving up the stew.

Warren sat down at the table and put his head in his hands. 'I really believed that this nonsense would be forgotten once Bannister was dead,' he mumbled.

*   *   *

It was early afternoon when Neil rode into Newberry. He was glad he was on his own because he'd woken up late, sharing the bed of the pretty whore, and even now he was still suffering the last effects of a hangover. He would never have heard the last about either from Cobb.

Cobb was one of those annoying people who seemed able to drink as much as he liked and never have a hangover, but then he was also one of those even more annoying, sensible, people who never drank any more than he could handle. Even worse he was always up bright and early and eager for action.

Not knowing where Cobb was now, Neil decided to stable his horse and then visit the marshal. He knew one of the first things Cobb was going to do was find the jailhouse, to introduce himself to the lawman and to talk to Steadman.

Not that Neil was happy about going into a jailhouse all by himself. Supposing he didn't come out again? And when he saw the almost completed gallows in the yard he gulped nervously and quickly looked away. He was aware that if it hadn't been for Cobb taking him on he could by now have ended up dangling from the end of a rope, either as a result of a judge and jury finding him guilty of robbery or, more probably, at the hands of a lynch mob.

Inside, Marshal Jackson sat at his desk while Bob Sparks was dealing out a pack of cards for a game of solitaire.

'Oh yeah, Cobb said to expect you,' Jackson said. 'He's got you a room of your own at Mrs Penrose's boarding house.'

Neil was as glad as Cobb that they weren't sharing a room. Although he denied it Cobb snored.

'Is he around town at the moment?'

'No. He rode out early this morning.'

'D'you know where he's gone?'

'One of the first people he meant to call on was Mr Rowlands at The Flying R.'

It was a relief that Cobb wasn't around to learn what time Neil had reached Newberry but it was even more of a relief that he hadn't gone to the Double D by himself, and without a warning. Neil wondered whether to say anything about the ranch and the Drake brothers to Jackson but decided not to in case Cobb didn't want the marshal to know everything that was happening.

'OK, I'll go down to the boarding-house and wait for him there,' Neil said, thinking he could also find somewhere to have something to eat.

Just as he reached the door, it opened and Amy Mallory came in. Jackson introduced them.

'Pleased to meet you, Neil,' she said, in her forthright way.

'Have you come to see Steadman?' Jackson asked, reaching into his desk drawer for the keys.

'Yes.' Amy smiled, but she couldn't hide the misery in her eyes. 'Neil, when you see him perhaps you'd tell Mr Cobb that Greg and I've been asking around town over who might have started rumours about me and Bannister.'

Jackson glanced at Sparks and both men tried not to grin. How on earth had Amy managed to get her brother to ask anyone anything!

'Everyone seems to have heard them but no one knows, or at least won't admit, to knowing who started them. Or why. Mrs Penrose is one of those who spread the word.' Amy reddened, from embarrassment at having to speak about such personal matters and anger at being linked to Ralph Bannister.

'She surely is a gossip,' Jackson agreed. 'And eager to believe the worst of people.'

'The trouble is she passes on so many tales she never remembers who told her them in the first place. But tell Mr Cobb we'll keep asking.'

Jackson opened the door to the cells. 'Take as long as you like.'

'Thank you.'

'She's a nice young woman,' Jackson said, once she was out of earshot.

Sparks nodded in agreement.

'I don't know what she'll do once Steadman is hanged. Shame. Pity he couldn't've given up his line of work and joined her and her brother in the livery business. I know they offered.'

'Some people like excitement and danger in their lives,' Neil said, thinking of Cobb.

10

'Hey, barkeep, three more beers!' Peter Warren banged on the counter.

'Don't you think you've had enough?' Ed Chadwin glanced over at the group of six young farmers gathered together at a table under the windows.

They'd met up a few hours earlier and been drinking steadily ever since. Their voices had been getting ever louder and now they sounded angry and drunk, a bad combination as far as Chadwin was concerned. He wasn't all that fond of farmers anyway; they didn't spend as much money in his saloon as the ranchers and their men.

'Give me the beers.'

Chadwin shrugged. He'd tried to warn them. It wasn't going to be him who woke up with a thick head and churning stomach. And he'd noticed that they were all carrying guns. He didn't want damage done in his saloon but neither did he want the young fools turning their anger on him.

Peter carried the drinks back to where his brothers, Martin and David, sat with the three others. Except for Martin, they were all in agreement. They wanted to do something about the ranchers, right this very minute, but none of them knew quite what, now that Ralph Bannister was dead and no longer there to lead them.

'We're on our own,' Peter said. 'The others are like Pa, with Ralph dead they don't wanna know. They're running scared, hoping the problem will go away whereas we know it damn well won't.'

'We must act now.'

Thinking about Bannister and the way he'd been shot down, David said, 'First off we oughta do something to make that killer, Steadman, pay.'

'He's in jail, he's goin' to be hanged at the end of the week.' That was Martin. 'What is worse than that? He'll pay all right.'

He wished he hadn't come into town. Their father had expected them all to help him clear the field, and that's where he longed to be now, but his mother had asked him to accompany his brothers so he'd agreed. Not that he held out much hope that any of them would listen to him. He was the odd one out and always had been.

'Hell, Martin, talk is the damn Bellington's man who arrived yesterday is gonna get him off,' Peter said, banging his fist hard on the table causing it to wobble. 'We can't let that happen.' He drank half of his beer down in one gulp and coughed violently. When he'd recovered he went on, 'We'll be made laughing stocks and the ranchers will think they can get away with goddamn anything they like. Steadman must be punished for what he did. Not just to Ralph but for all the wrongs he's done to us. And if the law won't do it then we'll have to do it for ourselves.'

'Yeah, that's right. We'll hang the

bastard for sure.' David rose in his seat as if wanting to go and string up Steadman there and then. He swayed a bit on his feet and his voice was slurred.

'Don't be stupid.' Martin pulled his brother back down. 'That's lynch talk.'

His worst fears were coming true. He only hoped he could stop them doing something stupid, like marching over to the jail and trying to break Steadman out. Marshal Jackson was a reasonable man but he'd never stand for that!

'Too goddamn right.'

'I think you've both had too much to drink and we oughta go home.' He ignored the others' jeers.

'What the hell's the matter with you?' Peter asked. 'The ranchers lynch the farmers and no one does anything to stop 'em. Steadman killed Ralph in cold blood.' He shivered. 'You didn't see Ralph's body. I did.'

'Marshal Jackson did arrest Steadman.'

Martin need not have spoken as Peter went on, voice rising with anger.

'Only because he had to. Martin, the ranchers take our land from us. Cheat us every way they can. Like Ralph said we can't let the bastards get away with it. They do and we'll end up losing everything. And you know how hard Pa has worked to provide for us all. What will he and Ma do if they're kicked off the farm?'

'It won't come to that.'

'We've gotta let 'em know we mean business.' That was one of the other three.

'See what happens first before you go off and do anything rash.' Martin risked more jeers. 'I'm sure Jackson means to hang Steadman. Ain't he building the gallows?'

That at least gave Peter pause.

'Look,' Martin went on, before anyone else could speak, 'I don't like the idea of the ranchers doing us down without any reason, I certainly didn't like the cowardly way Ralph was shot from ambush and I agree that we must stick together. Fight back when it's necessary. But only then. We don't want to give Marshal Jackson any reason to arrest us. That'll only help the ranchers, not us.'

Peter sighed. He supposed his younger brother was right. He usually was, dammit! But it was difficult sometimes to just sit back and do nothing, especially when he was sure right was on his side.

'OK. For now. But I tell you, Martin, if it looks like Steadman is goin' to get away with killing Ralph I'll be the first in line with a rope.'

'And I'll be right behind you,' David added. He suddenly sounded sleepy while one of the others yawned widely, setting off everyone else.

Behind the bar, Chadwin was beginning to hope things were going to turn out all right. The farm boys weren't used to drinking, especially in the afternoon, and with another beer inside them they seemed to be calming down. Or rather, seemed to be at the stage where they would soon lose consciousness. He decided it would be best to let them sleep it off at the table rather than roust them outside.

That was when the swing doors opened and a group of young cowboys sauntered in.

Oh, lordy, no!

Each group immediately saw the other. The farm boys sat up straight, shaking off their stupor.

'Look who the hell's here,' one of the cowboys said loudly, nudging his friends. They started to whisper and laugh together. 'What are you doin' in Chadwin's? Don't you know none of your kind is wanted in town?'

'We've as much right to drink in here as you,' Peter said, temper flaring straight off.

'Don't,' Martin said, as dismayed as Chadwin.

'You damn sodbusters don't usually have money enough to buy drinks.'

'At least we own the land we farm. We don't have to work for wages.' David was quick and eager to join in.

'All right, boys, stop this, the lot of

you,' Chadwin said. 'There ain't no need for any fighting. Let's all try to get along.' He smiled brightly at the newcomers, although in his heart he felt he was fighting a losing battle. 'What d'you want?'

'Whiskey. We drink real drinks not beer.'

David slammed his glass down on the table, so that most of the beer in it slopped over the rim.

'Stop it,' Martin warned, catching hold of his arm. 'It's what they want.'

'Perhaps it's what some of us want as well,' David spat out, pulling away from his brother's grasp. 'Some of us ain't cowards.'

'There's more of them than there are of us.'

'So what? We're more'n a match for them.'

Martin sighed. He felt as apprehensive as Chadwin about the rapidly deteriorating situation.

11

'Are you sure those men were from the Double D?' Cobb asked Neil.

'No. Lenny and the others I spoke to had never seen either of 'em before. But that was the brand on their horses.'

'Of course,' Jackson said, scratching his chin thoughtfully, 'if they had been employed by the Drakes they could've left the ranch to go elsewhere and been out to make some money by robbing you.'

'They didn't have much with 'em,' Neil pointed out. 'And if they'd left the ranch what were they doing with two of the ranch's horses? I suppose like Lenny said they could've stolen 'em,' he added, answering his own question.

Jackson looked at Cobb. 'You think they were Lucan and Carter, don't you?'

'They were fortyish,' Neil put in.

'One was tall and thin and the other shorter with very little hair.'

'Yeah that sounds like them,' Jackson agreed with a nod.

Cobb smiled in satisfaction. His suspicions were proved correct. 'I'll need to find out more about the Drake brothers.'

'Even though it was their men involved in trying to shoot you that doesn't mean the Drake brothers were behind it.'

'I know.' All the same Cobb thought they probably were. And he also intended to find out why. 'Tomorrow me and Neil'll ride out to look at where Bannister was shot and then go on to speak to the Drakes.'

'I'll go with you,' Jackson offered.

The three men were sitting in the First Choice saloon, which was the largest and best saloon in Newberry's busy red-light district. Cobb had noticed three other saloons as well as a brothel, a dance hall and billiards hall. The name of the saloon was picked out in gold leaf on its two windows and swing doors opened on to a big room with a bar at the back, behind which shone glasses and bottles. There was a gambling area to one side and a couple of waitresses.

At this time of the afternoon the saloon didn't have many customers and the few in there seemed to be mostly townsmen and ranch owners.

'It ain't rowdy enough in here for the cowhands,' Jackson had explained. 'And it's too expensive for the farmers.'

Cobb waited until Neil fetched over three more beers, as well as some free hard-boiled eggs for himself, then leant back in his chair.

'One thing is worrying me. If I'm right about Lucan and Carter trying to kill me and Neil . . . '

Neil hid a smile. Cobb made it sound as if he was never wrong, which come to think of it, Neil admitted, he rarely was.

' . . . how did they know where and when we were arriving?'

Jackson reddened as if he felt Cobb was criticizing him.

'I didn't tell anyone,' he said defensively. 'But as you know, once he was convicted, Steadman asked me to send a telegram to Mr Bellington asking for help and then you sent a message back saying you were coming out by train. There was only one place you could get off. Look,' he shrugged, 'I know messages like that are meant to be confidential, but hell, you can't keep much quiet in a place like Newberry where everybody knows everyone else's business. And Steadman was news! Everyone wanted to know what he said, how he was holding up and when the hanging was due to take place. It wouldn't have been difficult to find out about you.'

'I guess not,' Cobb agreed, not sounding very happy. He finished his beer. 'Well, unless those two men wanted to kill us for some other, unknown, reason, it must have to do with why we're here.'

Jackson agreed.

'Obviously I wasn't meant to reach Newberry to investigate Bannister's killing and that must mean someone wants Tom to hang.'

'Yeah,' Jackson said. 'I wonder why.'

'Neil, we'd better . . . '

Cobb got no further. The swing doors slammed back making the bartender tut and one of the waitresses jump and nearly drop the tray of glasses she was carrying. Bob Sparks came in and spotting them hurried over.

'Bob, what's up?' Jackson said, getting to his feet.

'Thank God I found you, Marshal,' the man said, stopping to catch his breath. 'There's trouble.'

'Steadman?'

'No. It's down at Chadwin's saloon. A fight. Between some idiot farm boys and some bigger idiot cowboys. Chadwin sent someone to the jailhouse to tell you. He needs help.'

'OK, I'll deal with it. You go back and guard Steadman.' Jackson turned a worried face towards Cobb. 'This could be a trick to break Steadman out of jail or to lynch him.'

'I'll come with you. Neil, you go with Sparks. And be careful.'

'Chadwin's is the furthest saloon up the street,' Jackson said, as he and Cobb hurried out.

Cobb didn't need telling: men were crowding about outside, laughing and yelling.

With Cobb close behind him, Jackson pushed and shoved his way through the crowd, shouting at them to go home. Then they were through the saloon's doors. Chaos met their gazes.

The fight was still going on. More onlookers trapped in the saloon stood against the walls or sheltered behind the bar while Chadwin looked on helplessly. Tables and chairs lay broken. Glasses were smashed and beer had spilled everywhere. And ten or eleven young man were in the middle of the floor, punching, kicking, rolling about. One lay senseless at the end of the bar, his head bleeding, the dented spittoon with which he'd been hit lying nearby.

Luckily no one had yet resorted to drawing weapons but Cobb wouldn't have liked to bet on that remaining the case for much longer.

'Oh hell!' Jackson said.

'Do something!' Chadwin screamed. 'They've wrecked the place.'

'Let's stop this!' Cobb was suddenly eager to join in the fray.

As two of the fighters swayed near to him, he grabbed hold of the collar of the nearest — a farm boy — shoving him out of the way then pitching him out of the doors and into the street. He blocked the blow of the cowboy and let fly with his own punch. His fist caught the cowboy on the chin and he fell down and stayed there. Someone else came at Cobb but Jackson stepped between them and pushed the farmer away. The boy tripped over one of the shattered tables, landing in the middle of the chair-legs and glasses. He tried to rise but collapsed back down, eyes glazing over.

Together with Jackson, Cobb waded through the fighters: parting them, hitting and kicking, thrusting them away. Cobb was a good fighter never afraid to play dirty if he had to and by the time they reached the far side of the room, he and Jackson had succeeded in stopping the fight. Young men lay or sat, clutching at bloody noses, holding cut heads, glaring at one another still or looking sheepish.

'What the hell's goin' on here?' Jackson yelled, once he'd got his breath back. 'Who the hell started it?'

Chadwin came out from behind the bar to join him and Cobb. 'It was both their faults, Marshal. The farmers have been in here nearly all afternoon, drinking and getting angry and stupid. Then these cowboys came in and started a slanging match.'

'Which soon got out of hand,' another man added. 'Still it was a good fight while it lasted.'

'Who's that hurt over there?' Cobb indicated the young man lying motionless by the bar. He went over to him and turned him on his side.

'It's Martin Warren,' Jackson told him.

'He tried to stop his brothers getting involved and got hit from behind for his trouble.'

'Not by either of his brothers?' Jackson asked.

'Oh no. It was one of the cowboys, but I didn't see which one. Peter and David are over there. You,' Chadwin nodded at Cobb, 'hit Peter and knocked him out while David foolishly tried to take on two of the cowboys. He's the one with the blackening eye and a cut lip. Serves him right. It was him flung the first punch that started it all.'

'It looks like Martin is the only one badly hurt,' Jackson said, after glancing round at the rest of the young men. 'The others are suffering nothing but cuts and bruises. Best get the doctor to see to him.'

A man ran out of the saloon to do his bidding.

'What the hell are you going to do with 'em all?' Chadwin asked. 'Look at my place. They want locking up.'

'Aw, hell,' one of the few cowboys still standing moaned. 'We didn't mean no harm.'

'Shut up,' Jackson told him. 'Mr Chadwin, I couldn't agree more. And normally I'd march the whole lot down to the cells and throw away the keys. But not while I've got Steadman locked up and waiting to hang. He deserves privacy in his last few days on this earth.'

'They can't be allowed to get away with this.'

'They won't. Don't worry.'

Peter Warren got shakily to his feet and rubbed his swollen jaw. His mouth was bloody and he'd lost two teeth.

'We weren't doing nothing until these cowboys came in and attacked us like they always do,' he said. 'Look at what they've done to Martin. He didn't even

119

want to fight and now he's hurt and you're goin' to let 'em get away with it. It ain't fair. You always support the ranchers,' he accused Jackson.

'I'll pretend I didn't hear that,' the lawman told him.

'You were drunk, you should've left when I told you,' Chadwin said.

'That's right, it's always our fault.'

'Be quiet!' Jackson ordered, losing his temper with a furious shout. 'No one is goin' to get away with any of this. Not even you, Peter. Now go and see to your brother. God only knows what your pa will say when he finds out.'

A sulky look on his face, Peter went over to Martin, bending down by him. After a couple of moments he was joined by David, who held his ribs, face twisted with pain. They muttered together but no one took any notice.

'Mr Chadwin, I'll take the names of these fools and when the judge next comes to town he can deal with the lot of 'em. That OK with you?'

'Yeah guess so.'

Jackson turned to Cobb. 'I can manage now. I'll see you in the morning?'

'Yes,' Cobb agreed.

'Thanks for your help.'

Cobb nodded and smiled. Like most everyone else he rather enjoyed a good fight.

12

In the event Cobb rode out to Bannister's farm with just Marshal Jackson for company. Jackson was worried that with such a short time to go to Steadman's hanging feelings were running high between the farmers, who might lynch him, and the cowboys, who might rescue him. So Cobb told Neil to stay at the jailhouse to help Bob Sparks make sure neither happened.

Riding fast it didn't take the two men long to reach Bannister's farm. As they rode down the slope from the trail, Cobb looked at the cultivated fields leading away from the few buildings.

'Whatever else Bannister might have been, he was a good farmer,' Jackson said, as they came to a halt. 'Helped by the fact that he had water on his land.'

'The land certainly looks good enough that someone might well have wanted to take it from him.'

Jackson agreed with a little shrug.

'Where did you find the body?'

'Over here.' Jackson led the way towards the corral. 'It looked like he'd dismounted but didn't have time to do anything else before he was shot.'

'Who found the body?'

'Peter Warren. That was the young man in the fight yesterday.'

Cobb nodded to show he remembered.

'In the weeks leading up to the shooting, the Warren boys, Peter and David anyway not Martin so much, had become thick as thieves with Bannister. Peter was riding over to see Bannister to talk to him about what they should do next. He rode into town to fetch me and the doctor. Doc reckoned Bannister had been dead a couple of days.'

'And there wasn't much to see?'

'No. No useful tracks or anything. But I did discover where the ambusher lay in wait. Behind there.' Jackson pointed across the dry strip of ground to an outcrop of rocks. 'I'll show you.'

'How did you know that was where he waited?'

'Because that was the one place I did find something. Footprints and a cigarette end. Someone had been there for a while.'

'Just one person?'

'Yeah.'

'And there was nothing to show who that was?'

'No.'

Cobb immediately saw that the rocks made a good hiding place. A man could stay there, out of sight, until his quarry put in an appearance. And it wasn't far from the corral so that even a reasonable shot would have had no difficulty in finding his target. Bannister wouldn't have stood a chance.

'Where's the Drake brothers ranch from here?'

'Just over the ridge. About half a mile away. When Bannister moved in the ranch was here already, although it wasn't owned by the Drakes then. This land never belonged to the ranch which runs towards the foothills in the other direction. Of course, in the early days, the ranch's cattle could easily be driven to the waterhole because no one owned the land. As soon as he moved in Bannister strung up barbed wire.'

'I bet that didn't go down too well.'

'That it didn't.'

'Why didn't the previous ranch owners try to buy this land and the water?'

'I don't know. It was before my time. Maybe they didn't think there would come a time when the rest of the country would be so dry and suffering from lack of water.'

'But Bannister was here by the time the Drakes moved in?'

'Oh yeah.'

'So they couldn't have bought it legitimately.'

'Not 'less Bannister was willing to sell.'

Cobb rode his horse to the top of the ridge and came to a surprised halt. 'Come here,' he called. 'Look at this.'

'What is it?'

'Someone has already decided that the water on Bannister's land shouldn't go to waste.'

From here it was possible to see that a large section of barbed wire had been broken down and cattle had walked, or more likely been driven, through it. At least fifty or sixty head, enough to leave behind a trail as they made their way to the waterhole and the good grass that surrounded it.

'Oh hell.' Jackson pushed his hat to the back of his head. 'Now, Mr Cobb, has that been done by accident or on purpose?'

'That, Owen, is the question. I think we'd better ask the Drake brothers, don't you?'

'Yeah. They could be the only ones responsible.'

★　★　★

Red-faced with fury, Fred Warren pulled the buckboard to a halt outside the doctor's surgery. He leapt down and without even bothering to secure the horses to the hitching rail marched towards the building.

'Oh-oh, here's Pa,' Peter said nervously.

The doctor beat a hasty retreat; let them all get on with it, he thought.

As soon as he saw Peter and David, Warren yelled, 'You bloody fools!'

'It wasn't our fault,' Peter began, but Warren shouted him down.

'Yeah, it was. You came to town looking for trouble. You should've been at the farm helping me. Then none of this would've happened. Instead, look at your brother!' He swept his hand towards Martin, who lay, still groggy and feeling sick, on the narrow bed the doctor kept for his patients. 'Your brother is hurt. He could've been killed!'

'We're sorry,' David mumbled.

'Sorry!' Warren flung his hat at his son. 'I'll make you damn well sorry! As old as you are you aren't too old for me to paddle your behinds! Do you know how worried your ma was when you didn't come home last night? She thought you'd been arrested and locked up, or even shot! Have you any notion at all about how worried she'll be when we bring Martin home like this? Or don't you care? Do you just think of yourselves?'

'No, Pa . . . '

'What on earth will she say?'

Peter and David glanced at one another. They were scared of the consequences of what had happened. It was bad enough to face their father's wrath, but they were used to that, it was going to be far, far worse to face their mother's distress.

'Oh, for God's sake, you make me sick the pair of you! Now help me with your brother, and be careful! Don't hurt him even more, and let's go home. Think yourself lucky nothing worse happened and think about the time when Marshal Jackson makes you face the judge. Don't think for one minute that I'm paying your fines for you! Come on.'

★ ★ ★

Neil wasn't any too happy about being left in the jailhouse — it was giving him the shivers — but he knew better than to argue with Cobb. And Sparks was glad of his company, especially when he kept beating him at cards.

'Marshal stayed here last night,' the old man said, pouring them both some coffee. 'Luckily no one tried nothing stupid. And I doubt there'll be any trouble today, although as some of those idiot farmers are still in town it might prove different tonight, once they get likkered up again.' He shook his head. 'I don't like it, Neil. We ain't never had a lynching here, but then there ain't been this upset before. The townspeople and the ranchers have always been on the same side against the outlaws or Injuns. Now everyone seems at odds with everyone else.'

'I'm sure Mr Cobb will sort matters out.'

'I hope so.'

Sparks sounded doubtful and despite what he said Neil was doubtful as well. There was so little time left.

Mug of coffee in one hand, Neil went to the door and stared across the plaza. All he could see was people going about their business. Across the way an older man was helping Peter and David Warren carry their brother to a buckboard. They laid him in the back. The man must be Fred, the father. He looked absolutely furious.

No trouble was stirring. But Sparks was right. There was an atmosphere in the air. Not just excitement at the thought of a hanging but an ill-tempered tension.

He wondered what Cobb would find out and what he would do if he didn't find anything. Cobb believed Steadman was innocent. Would he, a man to whom the law was so important, take the law into his own hands and break

Steadman out of jail or would he decide to let an unjustified hanging go ahead? Neil thought that Cobb wouldn't be happy with either alternative.

Nor would he be happy at the thought of failure.

13

Cobb was impressed with the Double D. Not as big as Rowlands's place, there was still plenty of work going on and the men around the ranch headquarters looked busy. The buildings appeared sturdy and well kept.

As he and Jackson dismounted before the house, the door opened and two men came out. They shut the door behind them, making it clear they weren't about to invite their visitors inside out of the sun.

'Allan and Reggie,' Jackson said, in an aside.

'Let's see what they have to say, especially about Lucan and Carter.'

As they approached, Reggie looked at them both with an insolent stare while Allan's forehead was wrinkled with an agitated frown.

Reggie's hand also hovered over the

gun he wore in a fancy holster.

So Cobb pushed his coat back to show that he too was armed and wouldn't be slow or afraid to use his Colt. Knowing his unspoken threat hadn't worked, Reggie looked put out and dropped his hand to his side.

'Marshal,' Allan said by way of welcome. 'To what do we owe this visit?' He turned to look at Cobb.

'This is Zachary Cobb from Bellington's Detective Agency,' Jackson said. 'He's here to ask some questions on behalf of Tom Steadman and his trial — '

'We don't know nothing about that,' Reggie interrupted. 'Except he's a disgrace to the ranching tradition.'

Cobb stepped forward. 'But your ranch is next to Bannister's farm and two of your men testified against Steadman didn't they?' No response. 'A Ben Lucan and Adam Carter, so I'm told.'

Cobb didn't miss the glance the two brothers gave one another.

'Are you calling them liars?' Reggie demanded.

'No. But I'd like to talk to them. Find out for myself exactly what they saw and what they say.'

Allan Drake pushed Reggie out of the way and nudged him in the side. 'Ain't possible, I'm afraid,' he said in a more reasonable tone.

'Why not?'

'They ain't here.'

'Where are they then?' Cobb didn't like the attitude of either brother and he was keeping his temper with some difficulty. They obviously considered themselves extremely clever and believed he and Jackson wouldn't notice, or understand, their glances and nudges.

'They've gone.'

'Yeah, but where?'

'Don't know.'

'Are you expecting them back?'

'Ain't none of your business.' Reggie spoke belligerently.

'I could make it my business.'

'Look, there ain't no need for

trouble,' Jackson said. 'Mr Cobb's questions seem reasonable to me so why don't you answer him reasonably?'

Reggie muttered something about hiding behind a badge but he subsided when Allan gave him a warning glare.

'Marshal, Mr Cobb, I apologize for my brother. Reggie might sound a bit rude but it's because we're annoyed with the two of 'em.'

'Why?' Cobb asked.

'They were always troublemakers and never did much work so I had to fire both of 'em. They left, what, a couple of days ago. We were glad to see the back of 'em. Ain't that right Reggie?' Reggie nodded. 'But the bastards stole two of our horses at the same time.'

'You didn't report it to me,' Jackson said.

'It's our problem not yours. And you're just the town marshal after all. You wouldn't've done anything.'

Somehow Jackson ignored the insult.

Allan shrugged. 'The two of 'em have gone. Never to return I guess. They're probably miles away by now.'

'Really?' Cobb said, thinking that, yes, it was unlikely the two men would come back seeing that they were dead and buried.

'Yeah, really and truly, Mr Cobb,' Reggie said. 'Anyway what're you asking all these damn stupid questions for? Our men told the truth at Steadman's trial. They might've been work-shy but that don't mean they're liars. They saw Steadman on Bannister's land the very day the stupid bastard was shot and they told the judge so.'

'Reggie, shut up,' Allan warned.

Reggie took no notice. He stepped forward. 'You ain't welcome here.' He pointed a finger at Cobb.

Cobb stepped back before Reggie could poke him in the chest, because that would be an insult he couldn't let go by. He did manage to pretend not to see the man's smirk as he obviously thought the private detective was a coward and was scared of him. Cobb had no doubt he could handle both of these men with no difficulty whatsoever but it was stupid to get into a fight over nothing. And it was sometimes best to give enemies the wrong impression, that way they might become over-confident and be even easier to defeat.

Jackson glanced at Cobb and tried not to grin. If the Drakes thought the man was a coward then that made them incredibly foolish. He said, 'By the way, Mr Drake, did you know a section of barbed wire on to Bannister's land is busted and some of your cows are getting through?'

Allan's eyes widened. 'Why, no Marshal! Has that happened? Really? God, no we didn't know. How awful.'

'Best get your cattle back on your own land and mend the fence.'

'Why should we?' Reggie demanded. 'Ain't no one on that land no more. Our cows have as much right to the water as the next man's.'

'It's not yours. And while there might not be anyone on the land at the moment that doesn't mean someone else won't buy it.'

'Some other sodbuster you mean?'

'Likely.'

'Don't worry, Marshal, we'll see to the problem without delay.'

'See you do.'

'For a town marshal you surely do poke your nose in business that ain't nothing to do with you.'

Jackson's face reddened with anger. No way was he going to ignore that. 'I might be the town marshal but I'm still a lawman deserving of respect and, Reggie, you'd do well to remember that. Now, Mr Cobb, perhaps we oughta go.'

'I'm sorry,' Allan said. 'But we really can't help you.' And he pushed his brother into the house before he could say any more and shut the door in their faces.

'Idiots,' Jackson said, still simmering with anger. 'I wish they'd give me an excuse to run 'em in.'

'Guilty idiots too,' Cobb said with a

glance back at the house.

But how to prove it?

★ ★ ★

'You fool,' Allan said to his brother once he'd watched Cobb and Jackson ride away. 'When will you learn? That big mouth of yours will get you, get both of us, into trouble one of these days. Why don't you keep quiet?'

'Aw hell, quit worrying, there ain't nothing to worry about,' Reggie said with a laugh. 'You saw how I bested Cobb. One threat from me and he backed down. I can handle him all right. He's nothing special. He didn't even dare come out here alone.'

Allan had seen the look in Cobb's eyes. He wasn't quite so sure. 'Do you think he knows about Lucan and Carter?'

'How can he?'

'Well, something has happened to them. Where are they? I wonder if Cobb had anything to do with their disappearance? No, he couldn't, could he? He was asking where they were.'

Reggie shrugged. He didn't care about a couple of cowboys and he wished Allan would stop whining on about them. He poured himself out a glass of whiskey and, turning to his brother, gave him a triumphant grin.

'I've come up with an idea.'

Allan groaned. Reggie's ideas seldom worked out as he hoped. In fact they usually went disastrously wrong.

'What is it?'

'Never you mind, not for now.' Reggie wasn't about to tell Allan, who would be sure to pour cold water on his plans. 'But I know how to sort this out once and for all. And it'll mean Cobb running back to Bellington's with his tail between his legs! And you'll get what you want too. Just wait and see.'

14

When Cobb and Jackson got back to Newberry it was the middle of the afternoon. Jackson, who was still furious over how the Drakes had spoken to him, rode down to the red-light district to find out if all was quiet and Cobb went to the jailhouse. Neil was playing cards with Sparks, and losing by the looks of things.

'Everything OK?' he asked.

'Yeah, Mr Cobb. How did you get on?'

'I'll tell you later over dinner. Right now I'd like to talk to Tom.'

Sparks stood up to unlock the door to the cells. Cobb beckoned Neil to follow him.

When he saw them, Steadman came to the door of his cell. He gripped at the bars then put his hands behind his back where they were out of sight.

'Hallo, Tom.'

'Zac, what's happening? You getting me out?'

'Not yet.' Cobb saw the hope die in the man's eyes even though he tried to hide his dismay beneath a shrug. 'Tell me what you know about the Drake brothers.'

'Allan and Reggie? Not a lot. They're newcomers to the area and I've only been out to their place a couple of times. But they seem OK ranchers to me. They know what they're doing. They joined the Cattlemen's Association almost as soon as they arrived and have attended most of the meetings since.' Steadman grinned. 'I don't think Mr Rowlands and one or two of the older ranchers like them much.'

'Why's that?'

'They have the tendency to shoot their mouths off. And they're always bragging about how important they're going to be. Why, what's your interest in them?'

Cobb didn't answer but said instead,

'And what about their two hands, Lucan and Carter?'

'Apart from the fact that they testified against me at the trial and goddamned lied, I don't know anything at all about 'em. I never had any kind of run-in with 'em — I ain't sure I'd even seen 'em before my trial — so why they stood up and lied I don't know. To be honest I was surprised they knew who *I* was. Why?' he repeated.

'Because they tried to ambush Neil and me at the railroad halt.'

'What?' Steadman sounded shocked. 'Why didn't you tell me before?'

'Because at first I wasn't altogether convinced it had anything to do with you.'

'But now you are?'

'Yes.'

'What happened?'

'Unfortunately they wouldn't surrender and I had to shoot the pair of them before I could ask them any questions.'

'But why would they do that?' Steadman paused then said, 'On the

143

orders of the Drakes, do you think?'

'I believe they were put up to it by the Drakes, yes, even though according to Allan and Reggie they were fired from the Double D and left a couple of days ago taking two of the ranch's horses with them.'

'But why . . . ?' Steadman began and then stopped.

'Because, of course, the Drakes were responsible for shooting Bannister so they could take over his land, or at least his waterhole. Some of their cattle have already been driven through a conveniently broken section of fence. And they didn't want me to reach Newberry to look into this case and perhaps find evidence that you're not guilty.'

'Or find something to show they were the ones shot Bannister,' Neil put in.

Steadman nodded. 'I know I didn't really want a rancher to be responsible for a cold-blooded killing but lately I've come to realize that was stupid of me. Some ranchers are as ruthless as the next man.'

Cobb was pleased Steadman had come to that conclusion.

'And, Zac, what you say makes sense. The Double D was suffering badly from this drought. Come to think of it when the Drakes first moved in they immediately started to make noises about buying Bannister out. They weren't happy because Bannister refused to let them drive their cattle across his land to the waterhole.'

'What happened then?'

'Mr Rowlands warned them to be careful, that Bannister's ownership of the land was legal. Reggie huffed and puffed a bit but pretty soon all went quiet. I guess they didn't do any more about it because if they had Bannister would've been only too ready to complain to Mr Rowlands if he felt he was being pressured.'

'But none of this came out at your trial?'

'Why should it?' Steadman asked. 'As I say nothing more happened and I forgot all about it. And, as it took place, what five months ago? I'm not sure if the judge would've considered it relevant anyway. It's still not proof that would stand up in court that they were the ones who shot Bannister. Or ordered it done. And why should the Drakes blame me?'

'You were a convenient scapegoat,' Cobb said, with a little shrug. 'Or is there any other reason?'

'None I can think of. So, Zac, how will you find the necessary proof, especially with Lucan and Carter dead and buried?' Steadman made an obvious effort to keep the anxiety out of his voice. 'There ain't much time left.'

'I'll send a telegram to the judge who held your trial, asking him to stop the hanging at least until the matter can be investigated further.'

'Will he take any notice?'

'I think there's enough evidence to at least cast a doubt in his mind about your conviction. Besides, Bellington's has an excellent reputation and he'll

146

know I know what I'm talking about.'

'I certainly hope he agrees.'

'He will.'

But Cobb looked worried as he and Neil left Steadman. As they started back towards the boarding-house where he was going to write out a message for the judge, he said, 'What I told Tom was right but whether Judge Bowyer thinks the same is another matter. Even if he does will the message get through in time? God knows where he is now. And the hanging is in two days' time.'

'If you don't hear anything will Marshal Jackson agree to postpone the hanging anyway?'

'I doubt it. He agrees with me that the case isn't as clear cut as he once believed, but like he says there's no evidence against the Drakes and I'm not sure he's truly convinced of their guilt. I don't think he'll have any choice but to go ahead with what the court decided. I don't blame him. He can't go against the law just on my say-so. And he has to live here amongst these people most of whom will want the hanging to take place.'

'Especially the farmers. Mr Cobb,' Neil paused. 'What will you do if the judge doesn't reply in time? Or if he doesn't agree with you?'

'I really don't know.' There was doubt in Cobb's voice for about the first time since Neil had known him.

'But if Steadman is innocent — '

'Which he is.'

' — then how can you let him be hanged?' Neil swallowed nervously at the thought. He wasn't happy with all this gallows talk!

'I can't, can I? And that's my difficulty.'

Neil hesitated, wondering how Cobb would take what he was about to say. It seemed sensible to him but then Cobb wasn't him. 'You could break him out of jail.' To his surprise Cobb didn't shout at him for suggesting such a thing and his next words told Neil that he too was at least considering the same.

'Then, dammit, I'd be breaking the

law. And supposing I'm wrong?'

'But you're not.' Neil had never seen Cobb so undecided. The man usually made up his mind what to do and then did it.

'No, I'm not. Hell!'

15

Reggie Drake rode into Newberry feeling pleased because he'd come up with this plan all by himself. Probably Allan would say he'd be a fool to attempt it and would try to stop him. If he was successful, and Reggie had few doubts on that score, it would stop Allan worrying; when Allan worried he was a real pain. No, once this was done their problems would be over. They could get on with their lives and important ambitions. It wasn't fair they should be held back by anyone, let alone a nobody like Tom Steadman.

Reggie dismounted by the livery stable and led his horse into the corral. He had timed his arrival in town well for it was still too early to put his plan into action. He would have to wait until it was dark and not many people were around the plaza, thus he could visit the brothel first where Madam Josephine's new girl would be waiting for him.

Amy Mallory came out. She didn't look particularly pleased to see him.

'Afternoon, Miss Mallory,' he said, tipping his hat to her and acting polite. 'Look after my horse, will you?'

'How long will you be?'

'I'll be leaving sometime this evening.'

'All right. He'll be ready for you.' Amy took hold of the horse's reins.

Reggie never knew when it was best to keep quiet and now with a wink and grin, he said, 'Good. I might have to leave in a hurry so keep him saddled and bridled.' With a spring in his step and whistling a lively tune he walked away leaving Amy wondering what he meant.

★　★　★

'You don't mind helping Bob Sparks guard the jail, do you?' Cobb asked Neil that evening, when they were finishing dinner at the boarding-house.

151

Neil wasn't best pleased at the thought but Cobb was so anxious over everything that he said, ''Course not. D'you think there'll be any trouble?'

'I doubt it. Not with a legal hanging only a couple of days away. But you never know and Jackson was worried earlier because a bunch of farmers was still in town and he was afraid things might get out of hand. Have you finished?'

'Yeah.' Neil gulped down the last of his coffee.

'Let's go then.'

The stores around the plaza were shut up for the night and the only lights were those showing from the hotel and the marshal's office. The few people about were heading for the saloons.

'Mr Cobb, which of the Drakes d'you think shot Bannister?'

'I don't know. Unless they confess' — which Cobb thought unlikely — 'I doubt we ever will know. Maybe Tom was right when he said they might not

have actually done the killing themselves but ordered it done. I reckon it
could have been Lucan or Carter. They
were quite ready to kill from ambush.'

They were almost at the jailhouse
when several shots fired in quick
succession rang out, loud and startling
in the stillness.

'Quick!' Cobb led the way at a run.

A moment later the jailhouse door
was flung open and Jackson came
rushing out.

'Someone shot at Steadman!' he
called. 'Round the back.'

'Neil, go help Sparks,' Cobb ordered.

While Neil hurried to do as he was
told, Cobb, together with Jackson,
raced round the side of the jailhouse
past the almost completed gallows.

At the back of the cells was a small
exercise yard enclosed by a high wall.
As they reached the rear of the jail
someone clambered over the wall and
jumped down.

'There!' Cobb said. 'Hey you! Stop!'

With a quick glance over his

shoulder, the figure took off, heading for the nearest alley. Cobb and Jackson started after him.

'Careful,' Jackson warned, as they reached the black mouth of the alley. He peered round the edge. Nothing and no one. 'It's OK. C'mon.'

'Where can he go?' Cobb asked.

'Anywhere. These alleys all lead into one another. Watch out!'

A movement up ahead. The flash of gunfire. Followed by shots. Bullets whined by them, slammed into the walls and ricocheted away.

Cobb threw himself to one side. He clawed out his gun, firing back even though he didn't have a clear target. From opposite him, Jackson gave a little cry and was flung off his feet.

'You hit?'

'Yeah,' Jackson muttered from the ground. 'Not bad though.'

The firing stopped and telling Jackson to remain where he was, Cobb went in pursuit. But by the time he reached the end of the alley and inched his way round the corner he'd lost sight of the man he was pursuing. He came to a frustrated halt. Whoever it was had gone. He could see no movement and hear no sound. As several alleys opened off this one he realized there was little use in trying to find the man who could be anywhere by now. Or could be waiting in the darkness to shoot at him. Swearing, he holstered his gun and went back to where he'd left the marshal.

Jackson was on his feet and holding his arm. As Cobb approached he said, 'Did you catch him?'

'No.' Cobb didn't like admitting that. 'Did you recognize him?'

'Unfortunately, no. He was too far away and it's too damn dark.'

'I think he also had a bandanna pulled up over his face. He was tall is about all I can say for sure.'

'It could've been anyone. At a guess it was one of the farm boys who're still in town. I'll go on down to the saloons later on and speak to them about it.'

'Want me to come with you?'

'No. This is town business and I'm town marshal and I can handle it by myself. Not that I expect to learn anything,' Jackson added gloomily. 'They'll all stick together and deny responsibility.'

'It might have been one of the Drakes.'

'Maybe.'

'What about your arm?'

'It hurts like hell but I'll manage.'

'OK. Was Tom hurt?'

'I don't know. When Sparks and me heard the shots and realized what was happening I immediately came outside to see if I could catch the attacker. I didn't stop to look in on Steadman.'

'We'd better find out.' Cobb wasn't sure what he would do if Steadman had been shot dead, except that he'd make sure he discovered who'd done it and make them pay. 'Get you patched up as well.'

As they emerged onto the plaza, they saw that quite a crowd had gathered in front of the jailhouse, demanding to know what was going on. Sparks was attempting to send them on their way but no one was taking any notice of him.

'It's all right, folks,' Jackson said, stepping up onto the sidewalk. 'Fun's over. Someone took a shot at Steadman and — '

'Hell he ain't dead, is he? We don't wanna miss out on a hanging.'

This caused some laughter and shouts of agreement.

'No, he ain't hit,' Sparks said, with a little nod of reassurance at the marshal.

'All of you can go on home now.' Jackson stood at the jailhouse door. 'Whoever did it is long gone.'

'And someone fetch the doctor,' Cobb added. 'The marshal has been shot.'

Inside the office, Jackson sat down as if his legs would no longer support him. He took off his shirt. The sleeve was soaked with blood and the wound was still bleeding.

'I don't think the bullet is in there,' he said.

'No,' Cobb agreed, 'but it's a nasty gash all the same. Go on home after you've been down to the saloons. Take it easy. Me and Neil'll stay here for the night. Make sure nothing more happens.'

'OK, thanks.'

Cobb went through to the cells where Neil stood guard outside Steadman's cell. Steadman was pacing up and down, looking both scared and angry.

'Catch him?' Neil asked.

Cobb shook his head. 'What about you, Tom, are you all right?'

'Dammit all to hell, of course I ain't!' the man shouted. 'Oh, I'm not hit but I'm sure shaken up. Someone wants me dead so badly they can't wait for the day after tomorrow! Three shots were sent through my window.'

'They missed,' Cobb pointed out.

Steadman clenched the bars. 'That's hardly the point. I want to know what that damn marshal intends to do to protect me.'

'You're not in any more danger tonight. Your attacker has run off.'

With an effort Steadman calmed down and grinned. 'I don't want to die before my hanging. I've got quite a speech prepared.'

Neil shuddered. How could he make jokes like that!

Cobb looked at the cell window. It was quite high up and meant that Steadman couldn't look out without standing on tiptoe and then he'd only just be able to see over the ledge. Whoever shot at him from the yard didn't have any better a view. He must have stood outside, reached up with a gun and fired wildly. He might have been lucky and have a bullet strike Steadman but he had no way of knowing where Steadman was or what he was doing. Whether he even had the right cell.

'Whoever the attacker was, he was a stupid one. It won't be too hard to find out who he was.' And Cobb just bet the marshal was wrong when he said a farmer was responsible and he was right about it being one of the Drakes.

★   ★   ★

Hair plastered to his head, neck clammy with cold sweat, Reggie Drake rode fast for home. He wasn't quite as pleased with himself as he'd been on the way into town. He didn't think he'd managed to shoot Steadman. He certainly hadn't heard a cry of pain or the fall of a body. Even firing through the cell window hadn't been as easy as he thought it would be — he hadn't even been able to see his target! Instead he'd nearly been shot himself. Nearly been caught. Had only escaped by luck.

What on earth was Allan going to say? There were times when Reggie knew he was the fool Allan considered him.

16

The doctor soon arrived to see to Jackson's wound. After a quick examination, he agreed that the bullet wasn't in the arm and, although there was a lot of blood, the wound was little more than a deep graze.

'It'll hurt and be stiff for a while,' he said, after he'd washed and bandaged the marshal's arm. 'But that's all. You're lucky.'

Jackson sighed in relief. It would be bad enough being shot and out of action at any time, right now with feelings running so high it would be disastrous.

'Try to take it easy for a couple of days,' the doctor added in warning.

'Easier said than done,' Jackson said with a little frown.

Once the doctor had left and the marshal had gone down to the red-light district, Sparks busied himself making coffee.

'I think I'll go pay a call on the Mallorys,' Cobb said, getting to his feet. 'They might have heard the shots and be worried. I'll try not to be too long.'

'OK.' Neil hid a little smile knowing that Cobb didn't like sitting about, doing nothing.

'And if Sparks thinks he can manage here by himself why don't you go along to the telegraph office, find out if there's a reply from the judge? Be quick though.'

'D'you think the attacker will come back?'

'I doubt it but I don't want to take any chances.'

The plaza was again quiet when Cobb went outside. Keeping a careful watch out for any possible ambush he hurried through the dark streets to the livery stable, where a lamp burned in the doorway. Both Greg and Amy were inside. When Cobb appeared, Amy turned to him, her face pale in the lamplight.

'Oh, Mr Cobb, we heard firing and Greg went to find out what it meant. He said there was an attack on Tom. He's not hurt, is he?'

'No, don't worry. Whoever it was missed.'

'Thank God.'

'But Marshal Jackson was wounded.'

'Oh no! What happened?'

'We chased the attacker but he shot Jackson and got away from me amongst the alleyways. Luckily Owen wasn't badly hurt.'

'Know who it was?' Greg asked.

'Not for certain.'

He and Amy glanced at one another.

'What is it?'

'Reggie Drake was in town this afternoon,' Amy said. 'He arrived about five o'clock and he was acting most strangely. Well, even more strangely than he usually does.'

Cobb tried not to grin. He'd felt sure he was right when he said one of the Drakes was responsible for the attempted shooting.

'He seemed excited as if he had something on his mind and he wanted his horse kept saddled and bridled because he thought he might have to leave quickly. He rode away not long ago. I didn't see him. But Greg did. Go on, Greg,' — she nudged her brother — 'tell Mr Cobb.'

'That's right,' was all Greg managed.

'And was he in a hurry?'

'Yeah,' Greg said with a quick nod and added in a mumble, 'Rode off real quick.'

'It's unusual for Reggie to leave this early,' Amy went on. 'He usually stays the night.' She blushed slightly, so Cobb realized that she meant Reggie slept at the brothel, while Greg frowned at Cobb as if he was to blame. 'And why should he be in a hurry? It's not as if the girls he associates with are married or have steady boyfriends.' Another deeper blush.

Cobb nodded to show he knew what she was talking about and that she needn't say any more.

'And while I know Reggie likes to drink in the saloon, perhaps play a game or two of poker, he rarely does anything from which he'd have to run away. And how would he know in advance?'

'Did he say anything to you?' Cobb asked Greg, who shook his head.

'But he looked red-faced as if he'd been running, didn't he?' Amy urged.

'Yeah.'

'But, Mr Cobb, why would Reggie want to try to kill Tom?' Amy said in an anguished voice.

'Because I'm sure he or his brother shot Bannister. Perhaps Reggie believed that with Tom dead the whole matter would be over and forgotten and I would just go home.'

'Why?' Greg asked.

Cobb took that to mean why had the Drakes killed Bannister. 'I can think of a couple of reasons.'

'The land and the water?'

'Yes, Miss Mallory.'

'And are they the ones who spread

the lies about me and Ralph Bannister?' Amy asked, while Greg thumped one hand against the other.

'They must have been.'

'Well, it wouldn't be difficult. Just one word in Mrs Penrose's ear and the news would be all over town. But why?'

'I'm not sure. Perhaps Tom had upset them and that was one way of getting back at him. And it wouldn't surprise me to discover that they're also the ones who managed to start the rumours about the farmers rustling cattle and, on the other side, the ranchers being against the farmers for no good reason. And those about Tom suddenly becoming violent and terrorizing the neighbourhood.'

'I doubt that would be hard either,' Amy said. 'The ranchers and the farmers don't like one another and would be only too pleased to believe the worst of each other.'

Her brother nodded. 'See it all the time.'

'But, Mr Cobb, I can understand

them shooting Bannister for his land but these other things — ' Amy spread her hands. 'What's behind it all?'

'I imagine it's tied up with their ambitions to be the biggest and the best. Cause discontent of all kinds and the resulting chaos would make it easier for them to step in and take over more land. Land that belongs to the farmers and which they feel should be theirs by right. In the case of Bannister's land and its good water they obviously decided not to wait and so had him shot.'

'Certainly they both consider themselves important, don't they, Greg? Oh!' Amy suddenly cried while her brother took hold of her hand. 'It's bad enough to know Tom might hang but when you know who the real culprits are and that Tom is innocent it's much, much worse.' Tears came into her eyes. 'What will I do without him? You must set him free, Mr Cobb, please.'

'Bear up, Miss Mallory, I'm hoping there'll soon be a reply to my message to Judge Bowyer. Hopefully he'll agree that a new trial can be called.'

But Cobb was doomed to disappointment. When he got back to the jailhouse, Neil gave him a telegram.

'What does it say?' Cobb asked, before he remembered that Neil couldn't read or write.

It was from the judge's clerk. Judge Bowyer was travelling on his circuit and was in between towns. The clerk would leave an urgent message for Bowyer to contact either him or Cobb but he didn't expect the judge to reach the next town for a couple of days.

By which time Steadman would be hanged.

'Damn!'

'Are you going to pay the Drakes another visit?' Neil asked.

'I could. But there's not much point. Reggie isn't about to confess to trying to kill Tom. Nor, more importantly, to the shooting of Bannister.'

'Then Steadman hangs?'

Cobb took several turns about the

office and then swung back to Neil with an anguished look in his eyes.

'Neil, I can't let that happen. Not now. Not when I know he's innocent and who's guilty.'

'So what are you going to do?'

'I've got an idea and I just hope Tom and, more importantly, Jackson will agree to go along with it.'

17

At first, to Cobb's disappointment but not his surprise, it didn't seem as if Jackson would agree to what the detective suggested.

The following morning when Jackson came to the jailhouse, his arm was in a sling and he looked white-faced from pain and lack of sleep. Cobb sent Neil and Sparks out to get some breakfast and then told the marshal what he had in mind. Jackson looked at him appalled.

'You really expect me to just let Steadman go?' he said incredulously. 'What is it? You take me for a fool? Just because you think I'm wounded and unable — '

'No,' Cobb interrupted. 'I don't expect you to just let Tom go.'

'But you want me to agree to you taking him off some place so he can't be hanged. Ain't that the same thing?'

'No.'

'He'll go free . . . '

'That's not what I mean,' Cobb said, as patiently as he could. 'Shut up and listen.'

Jackson frowned at the other man. 'Go on then, tell me all about this brilliant idea of yours.'

'I believe there's enough evidence to show that Tom is innocent and the Drake brothers are guilty. Don't you?'

No reply.

'And I'm sure that once he hears what I have to say, Judge Bowyer will agree and order a new trial.'

'And supposing he doesn't?'

'Then Tom will have to face the hangman. The same as he will if a second trial goes against him.' Cobb sounded as if neither possibility was likely. 'But look at what I've uncovered. The Drakes want Bannister's land, they sent two men out to the railroad halt to kill me. Reggie Drake tried to shoot Tom last night. Doesn't all that sound suspicious to you?'

'Of course it does. Don't make me out to be stupid. I've already said I agree with you. More or less. But there's no proof.'

'That's what I need the time to get.'

Jackson went on as if Cobb hadn't spoken, 'And it seems wrong to set Steadman free after he's been found guilty and sentenced in a proper court of law.'

'That was then, before this other evidence, these doubts, turned up. Do you really want an innocent man to go to the gallows? Can you live with yourself if you allow that to happen?'

'No,' Jackson admitted unhappily.

'All I'm asking is that the judge be given the chance to look at the evidence and make a decision one way or the other, which he won't be able to do if Tom is hanged tomorrow. According to you Bowyer's a good man and a better judge, so don't you think he'll agree?'

'I don't know . . . '

'Look, Owen, I'm not trying to take

advantage of you or do you down in any way. I promise to stay with Tom and not let him out of my sight. And I promise to bring him back here if things go against him. I've already spoken to Tom and told him the same. He agrees. He won't try anything stupid. He knows this is his last chance, his only chance, and he wants to take it. I don't think you'd be pleased with yourself if you denied it to him.'

Jackson sighed again. He didn't like this. It went against his every instinct as a lawman but at the same time he thought Cobb was right. And he felt sure he could trust Cobb and what he said.

'OK,' he agreed at last. 'But you'll have to wait until tonight when it's dark and no one's around to see you.'

'All right. I agree.'

'Maybe in the meantime you'll get a reply from Bowyer.' Jackson rubbed a hand over his face. 'God! How the hell am I going to explain any of this to the town council, or to the judge? I'll probably be strung up in Steadman's place!'

'I'll take full responsibility.'

Although Cobb spoke confidently, he really wasn't any too sure how he was going to explain his actions to Mr Bellington or how his employer would react; hopefully he'd approve. But Cobb knew that would happen only if he was right and Steadman was proved innocent! He was going out on a limb for the man and his job, like Jackson's, was on the line.

'And I don't want you going far. I want you nearby.'

Cobb nodded in agreement. 'Any idea where I can hole up? It shouldn't be for long.'

Jackson thought for a moment or two. 'There's a line cabin out on Rowlands' land, near Simmons Creek. As far as I'm aware it's seldom used these days so no one is likely to come by. It's only a couple of hours' ride away. Steadman will know where it is. You should be safe enough there. But you'd best take some supplies with you because I doubt if any will've been left there.'

'I'll do that.'

'And, Mr Cobb, your assistant, Neil, stays here with me.'

'Agreed.' Cobb tried not to grin, wondering how Neil would take to being a hostage.

'He can help me when things get heated up as they will when everyone finds Steadman has gone and they're being denied a hanging. Hell! I can't believe I'm doing this!'

'It's the right thing to do. You know it is.'

'And you'd also better start to gather together proof that'll stand up in court.'

Cobb thought that was a good idea. But how?

★ ★ ★

'You did what!' Allan Drake exploded. 'You fool!'

Reggie looked sulky. He hadn't

intended to tell Allan about his failed attempted killing of Tom Steadman but his brother was bound to find out. Better hear of it from Reggie than from someone else. He'd thought about trying to deny he was responsible but Allan had a way of worming the truth out of him.

'It seemed like a good idea at the time. It would've been a good idea if it had worked.'

Allan stood up as if he was too irritated with Reggie to remain sitting down. 'But your ideas never do work, do they? Especially when you act alone without telling me. You never think things through properly.'

'That ain't fair.' Reggie looked and sounded sullen. To his annoyance Allan still had the ability to make him feel like a small boy.

'You always make a mess of things.'

Reggie said no more. The trouble was Allan was right. 'It's OK, no one saw me. I got clean away.'

He decided not to say anything about

talking to Amy Mallory when he arrived in Newberry. He couldn't keep his mouth shut and more than once Allan had threatened to shut it for him; this might be one of those occasions when he carried out his threat.

'I hope you're right.' Allan flopped down in his chair so he could finish his breakfast. 'I guess you must be or else the law would've been out here by now asking damn fool questions.' He picked up his knife and fork. 'Reggie, I don't like any of this. That detective, Cobb, already suspects us . . .'

'Cobb!' Reggie snorted, regaining some of his cockiness now his brother's anger was fading. 'Anyway, Steadman will be hanged tomorrow and the matter forgotten. Cobb will have to go back to wherever he came from and not be any the wiser.'

'Yeah, hopefully.'

Reggie poured out more coffee for both of them and then gathered up the plates, stacking them in the sink. 'Allan, we are going in for the hanging, ain't we?'

'Try and keep me away! I want to see that sonofabitch hanged for the way he talked down to us just because Rowlands didn't like us. As if he believed he, the Association's damn detective, was more important than us, two of the Association's best ranchers.'

'And for the way Amy Mallory preferred him,' Reggie added, with a spiteful grin.

Allan scowled and said nothing. He kept telling himself that tomorrow would soon be here. Surely nothing could go wrong between now and then.

18

To Cobb's relief nothing happened during the day to make Jackson change his mind.

People — ranchers, cowboys, farmers and their families — did start to arrive for the hanging and soon the hotel and boarding-houses were full up. Some of Newberry's citizens decided to take advantage of the situation by letting out a spare bedroom, or even their own bed, to the sightseers and charging exorbitant amounts. Cobb was fearful that Jackson would decide he couldn't face their wrath when they found Steadman had gone, especially as no message came over the telegraph from Judge Bowyer, but he didn't.

It was a long day for them all but thankfully at long last the stores closed, most people went home and the rest wandered down to the red-light district, which was doing a roaring trade. The plaza was quiet and dark.

Steadman had said he wouldn't leave unless Amy and Greg Mallory were told of the plan, as he didn't want Amy to worry unnecessarily. Greg was to bring two horses to the back of the jailhouse out of anyone's view, for the back of the jail wasn't overlooked. While they waited, Cobb took Neil to one side.

'Be careful,' he warned. 'And keep your eyes open. I'm expecting the Drake brothers to come to town for the hanging, everyone else has and it wouldn't look natural if they didn't. And they'll want to make sure he is hanged. Watch for their reaction when they realize Steadman has been spirited away. I'm not sure if they know you came to town with me but keep out of their way so they can't ask you any questions or threaten you. Let Jackson do any talking to them and to everyone else.'

'OK,' Neil agreed readily. 'How long will you be gone?'

'Only until there's a reply from the judge. Although if he does come back to hear what I've found out, I might keep Tom out of the way until Bowyer actually arrives. Perhaps until he agrees to a new trial.'

'You think the Drakes might try to shoot Steadman even if the judge agrees with you?'

'Maybe. Who knows? And whatever the judge decides it wouldn't do Tom much good if he'd already been shot by the Drakes! And, Neil, look out for Amy. If the Drakes were willing to blacken her name for reasons of their own they might be willing to use her to try to get at Tom.'

Neil nodded. He began to think he was going to have a lot to do, was being given a lot of responsibilities, and he hoped the judge would soon send a reply so Cobb could come back to deal with everything.

At that moment, Greg Mallory slipped in through the door. 'Horses are here,' he said gruffly. 'Supplies too.'

'Is anyone around?' Jackson asked, then realizing it was unlikely Greg would say any more he went to the door and peered out. He looked up and down the street; there was no movement. He handed the keys of the cell to Cobb. 'Get Steadman while I keep watch.'

'Good luck,' Neil said.

'You too.' Cobb went through to the cells. 'Tom, you ready?'

'Yeah.' Steadman joined him. 'Do I get a gun?'

'No. Don't push your luck. Come on.'

Jackson beckoned to them. 'It's OK.'

As soon as Cobb and Steadman were outside, Jackson closed the door behind them so they were in darkness.

'This way.' Cobb pushed Steadman in front of him. For a moment he had a fear that Jackson might have set them up, would have men in place to shoot Steadman for trying to escape and him for helping. But nothing happened.

Not rushing, bending low, the two

men kept close to the jailhouse wall. They walked through the yard beneath the shadow of the gallows to the back. The two horses waited there. Cobb let out a sigh of relief.

'It might be taking us out of our way a bit but we'll leave Newberry by the business district,' he said, for that too would be shut up for the night and no one around to spot them.

'Good idea,' Steadman agreed. 'We can circle round once we get out of town. I know the way.'

Slowly they rode toward the plaza. As they got there a couple of cowboys passed by on the other side of the road. They resisted the temptation to put spurs to the horses' sides and gallop away. Thankfully the cowboys took no notice. No one else saw them, no lights were suddenly lit, there were no shouts of discovery or alarm. They were free and clear.

'They're away,' Neil said, from where he was peeking out of the window.

'Thank God.'

To their surprise Mallory suddenly spoke up, 'I hope no harm comes to Amy through this.'

'It won't,' Jackson promised. 'I'll make sure of that.'

Greg nodded and left.

'Now what?' Neil asked.

'We wait. Sparks is walking round the saloons, keeping an eye on things down there, while I sit in here and pretend I'm still guarding Steadman. God,' Jackson wiped a hand over his face, 'I just hope I've done right.'

'I'm sure you have. Mr Cobb wouldn't have suggested it if he hadn't thought it was the proper thing to do.'

'There don't seem any need for you to be here as well, Neil, you might as well go back to Mrs Penrose's and get a good night's sleep.'

Neil was only too pleased about that. He had no wish to spend another night in the jail, even if it was in the office rather than the cells.

'If there's any trouble I'll come running.'

'And be here early tomorrow morning. The hanging is set for ten o'clock and that's when I'll need help.'

★　★　★

'Ain't no one coming after us,' Steadman said.

Cobb agreed. He'd looked over his shoulder several times but there was no pursuit.

'Won't take us long to get to the line shack. No one will think to look for us there. Zac, what happens now? Will you just wait for the judge's reply and hope what you've found out will be enough to convince him of my innocence?' He paused. 'Will it be enough?'

'I doubt he'll just accept my word, he'll want proof that'll stand up in court.' Might as well admit that.

'So, how are you going to find the necessary evidence? I must admit I can't think of any way.'

'I'm hoping that when the Drakes realize you've given them the slip they'll give themselves away by doing something stupid.'

'From what I hear Reggie has got quite a temper on him and is likely to act rashly once he learns he's been thwarted.' Steadman looked across at Cobb. 'I hope you ain't put anyone's life at risk by this.'

So did Cobb and he thought, again, that he was worried about leaving Neil in Newberry. Marshal Jackson was a good man but would he be able to handle the Drakes? 'What else was there to do?'

Steadman shrugged. 'Nothing I guess. Zac, there's one thing that's puzzling me.'

'What's that?'

'I can understand the Drakes causing trouble between the ranchers and the farmers in order to further their ambitions. And when that wasn't working fast enough for 'em shooting Bannister in order to steal his land and his water. I can understand them putting the blame on me. I was the obvious scapegoat and it probably suited them to have someone to blame rather than let Jackson search for the real culprit. After all he might well have come up with the truth.'

'But?' Cobb knew what Steadman was going to say.

'Yeah, but. What I can't understand is why spread lies about Amy and Bannister and me being jealous. OK, it gave me another reason to shoot Bannister, but the fact I was the Association's detective and they got two of their men to lie about having seen me in the area at the time of the killing, the same two who tried to kill you and Neil, would probably have been enough to get me convicted. So why bring Amy into it?'

'That's been puzzling me too.'

'It just seems so unnecessary. Nothing to do with the rest of it. And the rumours started some time before the killing. It doesn't make sense. I suppose it was them who spread the lies about her?'

'Who else? Everyone I've spoken to thinks highly of her. And Greg. It makes me think there's more behind the killing and blaming you than land and water rights.'

'But what?'

Cobb sighed. 'I don't know but if I did I'd have the answer to everything.'

19

Cobb was awake earlier than usual the following morning. He was too agitated to sleep. As he got up Steadman continued to snore in the line shack's other bunk. Although he wanted a cup of coffee, Cobb decided to wait rather than disturb him; for it was probably the best night's sleep Steadman had had in a long while. He stretched and crossed over to the door, inching it open. Dawn streaked the sky with blue, lighting up the line of low hills that followed the almost empty creek. Somewhere, not far away, a bird called to another but that was the only sound.

Not that Cobb was in any mood to appreciate his surroundings. He should have stayed in Newberry and let Neil come here with Steadman. Except that Jackson would never have allowed that. Cobb didn't like being away from the centre of things, he liked to be in on the action. And while he trusted Neil to do what he'd asked him to, at least to the best of his ability, that might prove to be not enough. More importantly, he didn't think it right that Neil should be in town where the danger might lie while he was out here, safe. Unfortunately, there was no choice. He would just have to sit and wait. And wonder.

Hell and damnation, what was happening in Newberry . . .

★   ★   ★

Uproar!

Neil was also up much earlier than usual. Which was partly because he knew Jackson was expecting him and partly because he'd had to share his bed with a stranger who'd come to town for the hanging and who'd twitched and turned all night long. The dining-room was also crowded, all the talk being about Steadman and how long it was until he stepped up on to the gallows and how he would behave once the rope was round his neck. Neil even hurried his breakfast and didn't ask for seconds mostly so he could be away before Mrs Penrose noticed Cobb was missing and asked him questions as to where he was; which, being nosy, she would do given the chance.

As Neil arrived at the jailhouse, Sparks opened the door and let him in, shutting and barring the door behind him. For once the old man was quiet. Marshal Jackson had taken off the sling he'd worn to support his wounded arm and was standing behind the desk flexing his hand and arm. He'd unlocked the gun cabinet that hung on the wall and taken out a couple of rifles. Now Sparks picked them up and made sure they were loaded and ready.

'Not that I intend shooting anyone,' Jackson said, in warning to Neil. 'Steadman might be innocent but so are the townspeople and the others. These guns are for our protection. So I don't want you getting trigger-happy.'

'I won't,' Neil said.

The hanging was set for ten o'clock. They had three hours to wait. A long while. Neil wished it was time already and this was over and done with.

But it quickly became obvious they wouldn't have to wait three hours because sightseers soon started to gather before the jail. Quickly the street was packed, other people hung from windows of nearby buildings, yet more had climbed up on to roofs.

They seemed to be divided into three groups: ranchers and cowboys on one side, farmers on the other and towns-folk in between. The mood was cheerful, everyone laughing and joking.

'That won't last long,' Jackson gloomily predicted. 'I'd best go out and face 'em. The longer I leave it the worse it'll be. Damn Cobb!' He picked up one of the rifles and handed the other to Neil. Sparks had already got hold of a shotgun. 'Ready?'

Neil and Sparks glanced at one another. They both nodded wordlessly and followed close behind as Jackson opened the door and stepped out on to the sidewalk.

They were confronted by a sea of faces. Jackson picked out a few. Some of the townsmen, members of the town council standing together with their wives. Hugh Rowlands with his wife close by. Fred Warren and his three sons, Martin still looking bruised and pale, Peter and David grinning with expectation. Louisa hadn't come in with them and Jackson wasn't surprised about that for she disapproved of violence of any kind. And there were the Drake brothers standing on the edge of the crowd. He would need to watch them.

'Folks, folks!'

Gradually the noise died away as everyone stopped what they were doing to stare at Jackson. He gulped nervously.

'Where's Steadman?' someone called. 'Bring him out.'

'When's the hanging?'

'There ain't goin' to be a hanging,' Jackson said. 'Not this morning anyway.'

There was a moment of deathly quiet then the shouts and questions began. The mood turned instantly ugly.

'Why the hell not?'

'Where is he? Don't say the bastard's died on us.'

'I knew it!' That was Peter Warren. 'Them damn ranchers have stuck together and gotten him out.'

'Hush, hush, let the marshal speak.'

'Yeah, let him explain. If he can.'

'Neil, see the Drakes' faces,' Sparks whispered. 'They sure as hell don't like this.'

Neil glanced their way. Sparks was right. Allan and Reggie both looked furious — and apprehensive.

Again silence fell. Ominous this time.

Jackson said, 'Mr Cobb, the detective from Bellington's Agency has found enough evidence to cast doubt on Steadman's conviction . . .'

More shouts of disbelief and disagreement.

' . . . He's sent a message to Judge

Bowyer asking him to reconsider the matter and until Bowyer replies, one way or the other, Cobb has taken Steadman out of town in order to keep him safe.'

'Steadman is guilty,' Reggie Drake yelled, to a chorus of agreement. 'He should hang. What right has that damn fool Cobb to say otherwise and for you to agree with him?'

'I don't want to see an innocent man hanged for the sake of a few days.'

'He ain't innocent.'

Fred Warren stepped forward. 'And what happens if Bowyer disagrees with this Cobb fella?'

'Then Cobb will bring Steadman back and the hanging will go ahead.'

'Oh yeah!' Yells of disbelief. 'Why should he come back?'

'He won't!'

'This is all a damn waste of time,' Reggie said. 'Steadman should be hanged now. Let's get him.'

A few people surged forward, fists were clenched and raised. Neil took a frightened step back then steadied himself. Jackson held up his rifle and fired over their heads. Everyone skidded to a halt.

'He's not here, I told you that. Rushing the jail won't do any good and might get some of you hurt.'

'Let's get the marshal instead!'

'Yeah!'

'No, stop, don't be stupid.' Fred Warren stepped up on to the sidewalk to stand by Jackson.

'Pa!'

'No, Peter, listen to reason. It don't seem right to me, but Steadman is gone. Maybe the marshal is right or maybe he's wrong. But attacking him won't do any good.'

'He's always on the side of the ranchers! He ain't no proper lawman!'

'Look,' Jackson said, 'I'm sure we'll receive a reply from the judge within the next couple of days.' He hoped so anyway. 'There won't be long to wait.'

'Where is Steadman?' Allan Drake asked.

As if, Neil thought, Jackson would tell him!

'Somewhere safe. If he's guilty I promise he won't get away with this. But I think he deserves a chance.'

It was evident few others did.

'I don't want any trouble over this.'

'Trouble is what you'll damn well get,' Reggie yelled.

'Yeah, yeah!'

'Go home now, all of you.'

Some of the crowd slowly, reluctantly, began to move away, the majority stayed where they were as if they couldn't believe what they'd heard. Small groups were formed, arguing amongst themselves, complaining about the marshal, grumbling about private detectives; wanting to do something. Others shouted and yelled and seemed ready to start flinging punches. Or worse. The members of the town council, all looking furious — this was bad for business — strode up to Jackson. They were closely followed by Hugh Rowlands.

'Jackson! We want a word with you! Now!'

'What's the meaning of this? How dare you take something like this on yourself.'

'Best come in.' With a little sigh, Jackson led the way into the jailhouse. 'Neil.'

'Yes, sir?'

'When you can, go on down to the telegraph office, find out if there's a reply from the judge.'

Neil had no wish to be present while Jackson was bawled out by the town council and he decided that the time was already right. Everyone was much too busy yelling and arguing amongst themselves to take any notice of him. Even so he kept to the quiet of the alleys as he sprinted down to the telegraph office, which was situated just beyond the livery stable. He reached it without being accosted.

But he found there was no good news.

'No, ain't no reply yet,' the operator

said. 'I think the line might be down somewhere.'

'Hell.' That was the last thing either Cobb or Jackson would want to hear.

'Soon as there's a reply I'll bring it to the marshal, don't worry.'

'OK, I'll tell him.'

Neil stepped out of the telegraph office. As he did so he heard a woman cry out from the direction of the livery stable.

It was Amy Mallory.

20

Neil broke into a run. Cobb had entrusted him to look after Amy and now it sounded as if she was being threatened, even hurt. Who by? One of the Drakes, Reggie most likely, or perhaps a farmer so angered that Steadman had escaped the noose he was willing to take that anger out on Steadman's girl. As Neil ran he eased his gun in its holster.

He'd learned caution from Cobb, so instead of bursting into the stables, he came to a halt outside the door and peered round it.

Amy stood in the middle of the floor, facing him, fear in her eyes. With his back to Neil, holding on to Amy's arm, body thrust towards her, was, surprisingly, Allan Drake.

As Neil stepped inside, Allan said, 'Where is he? You must know.'

'No I've told you, I don't.' Amy tried to pull away from the man. 'Let me go. You're hurting.'

'Tell me where Steadman is.'

'Let her be,' Neil said angrily. 'Like she says, she don't know where he is.'

With a snarl of fury Allan swung round. He thrust Amy from him, almost sending her toppling to the ground.

'Stop that!' Neil didn't like to see a woman being hurt.

'Stay the hell out of this,' Allan shouted.

He raised his arm and punched Neil in the chest. Neil fell backwards and hit against the door of one of the stalls. Allan marched up to him, fury contorting his face.

'So, kid, do you know where he is?'

'No.'

'Then you're of no use to me.' And the man drew his gun and pointed it at Neil.

'Don't!' Amy screamed and jumped at Allan, struggling with him.

His gun fell out of his hand and to the floor. Quickly Neil kicked it out of the way. Allan shrugged Amy off him, called her a nasty name, and shoved her so hard that this time she couldn't save herself from crashing to the ground.

Shakily, Neil got to his feet and drew his own gun. 'Stop this! Or I'll shoot you.'

Breathing heavily Allan looked at him, then at Amy who had sat up and was rubbing her arm. For a moment Neil thought he wasn't going to take any notice of his warning but then he took a deep breath and managed to calm down.

'I'm sorry, Miss Mallory.' He spoke in an imploring tone, holding out a hand towards her. 'I really didn't mean to hurt you.'

She refused to look at him.

'Amy, sweetheart, I love you. I always have.'

At this Amy did look up, eyes widening with surprise. 'But for some reason you seem to prefer that bastard,

Steadman, to me. You deserve better.'
When she didn't reply, Allan's face and voice hardened. 'I want you, Amy. I mean to have you.'

Still no reply.

'You haven't heard the last of this, either of you.' And Allan pushed by Neil and ran out of the stables.

'Miss Mallory, are you all right?' Neil holstered his gun and went over to her, reaching out a hand to help her up.

'I think so,' Amy replied, brushing down her skirt. 'He came in here and started demanding to know where Tom was. He wouldn't listen to me. I was quite scared of him. Thank goodness you came along when you did or I'm not sure what he might have done.'

'Where's Greg?'

'Earlier this morning Marshal Jackson asked if he would go down to the red-light district and help Bob Sparks patrol it once he'd broken the news Tom had gone in case there was trouble. We didn't expect trouble to come here.'

She tried to laugh but it was obvious to Neil she had been badly frightened. He didn't blame her. There had been something about Allan Drake that had frightened him as well, and not just because the man had tried to shoot him.

'Don't leave me, will you?'

'No, of course not. But I think the best place for you is the marshal's office. You'll be safe there.'

Amy nodded agreement. She picked up the gun Drake had left behind and shoved it in the belt of her skirt.

'Neil, did you hear what Allan said? That he loved me! What did he mean by that? Reggie is nearly always the one who leaves and collects their horses when they come to town. Allan rarely even comes to town and I don't think I've seen him in here above a couple of times. In fact I don't think I've ever exchanged more than a few words with him. How can he possibly love me?'

'Never mind about that. Let's go.' Neil didn't want to be caught alone with Amy if Drake decided to return. One hand on the butt of his gun and the other at Amy's elbow he led the way out of the stable. To his relief there was no sign of Allan, or Reggie.

In fact they saw no one until they came to the plaza. It was still full of people, all of whom appeared to be venting their outrage at the jailhouse.

'Oh!' Amy said in horrified surprise.

'Don't worry.' Neil pulled her close. 'Let's hurry.' He wondered if he'd made a mistake in coming here, knew that at the least he shouldn't have been in such a rush to get Amy to the jailhouse but should have followed the alleys again. It was too late to go back because some of the crowd had already turned and spotted them, were pointing and nudging their neighbours. They would be no safer going back to the stables, less, because at least Jackson was in the jail to help them.

They hadn't gone very far when suddenly Peter and David Warren stepped out in front of them.

'You're with that detective, ain't you?' Peter accused Neil.

'And you're Steadman's girl,' David added.

'This is nothing to do with Miss Mallory,' Neil said, trying to push by them.

'Steadman is a damn killer and you're helping that damn detective set him free,' Peter went on. 'And she's the killer's girlfriend. And you're protecting her.'

He raised his fists and Neil feared he was about to have another fight on his hands, one in which several of the people round about might join in.

'Peter!' It was Fred Warren. He shoved David out of the way and faced his eldest son. 'I know you're angry but I didn't bring you up to bully women. You should be ashamed of yourself.'

To Neil's relief Peter looked shamefaced.

'Let them be on their way.'

'I'm sorry,' Peter mumbled and stood aside.

Warren remained on Amy's other

side as they walked to the jailhouse.

'Thanks,' Neil said.

'Oh, I ain't doing it for you, I'm doing it for my boys. Steadman should've been hanged today.'

'But he didn't do it,' Neil said. 'And Mr Cobb knows who did and now I think I know why.'

'Who?' Warren demanded. 'Why?'

'I need to tell the marshal and Mr Cobb first.'

They were at the jailhouse door at last and Jackson opened it for Neil and Amy to go through, while Warren turned away to find his sons. Immediately Amy sank down on one of the chairs and put her head in her hands.

'It's so awful out there. I didn't expect this.'

'You're all right now.'

'Miss Mallory, are you OK? I shouldn't have left you alone.' Jackson made sure the door was locked and secure. 'Neil, what's happened?'

Quickly Neil told him.

'Allan Drake? Allan was threatening

Miss Mallory? It's hard to believe.'

'It's true and as he left he told Amy he loved her and that she deserved better than Steadman. It was as if he couldn't believe she could prefer anyone to him.'

'God!'

'It doesn't make sense,' Amy said, trying not to cry. 'Not Allan. I could believe it if Reggie thought he was in love with me. He thinks he's in love with most every woman he sees. But not Allan.'

'Don't you realize what this means?'

'No, what?' Both Jackson and Amy stared at Neil.

'Mr Cobb thought there might be more behind this than the Drakes wanting Bannister's land but he didn't know what. Well, now we do know, don't we?'

'Oh God,' Jackson said with a nod. 'Allan is in love with Miss Mallory. With Steadman dead he believes that not only will he and his brother be able to take over Bannister's land and water but that Amy will be free for him to woo.'

'Exactly.'

Amy turned pale. 'How can he? I won't . . . it's ridiculous!' She raised stricken eyes towards the two men. 'But if he loves me then why was he willing to blacken my name with rumours about me and Bannister? Was it just to cause more trouble for Tom?'

Neil thought about that. 'That was probably part of it but' — he'd seen the mad look in Allan's eyes — 'I reckon he just couldn't stand the thought of you loving Tom instead of him and so wanted to punish you for doing so.'

'And perhaps to try and get the pair of you to argue and fall out of love,' Jackson added.

'I'll tell him I don't care for him and never could and put a stop to this nonsense.'

'From the way Allan Drake was behaving I doubt he'd listen. Or be able to tell the truth from his imagination. He loves you and he obviously believes that given the chance you'll love him back.'

'But . . . '

'No, Miss Mallory, Neil's right. It won't do any good for you to approach him. It might make things worse and might put you in danger.'

'But we must do something.'

Jackson went over to the window and stared out at the crowds milling around in the plaza. 'Things won't quieten down for a while. I don't like to leave the town until they do but Mr Cobb needs to know about this. And quickly.'

'I could go,' Neil offered.

'You don't know the way.'

'I know the area,' Amy said. 'I could take Neil.'

'I'm not sure — '

Amy went on. 'Your job as town marshal means you should be here looking after the town. Keeping people quiet. You're the only one who can do that. Neil can't. Nor can Sparks and Greg. No one will listen to them.'

'Greg could go with Neil.'

'No, please, Marshal, I want to see Tom, especially now when the last piece of the puzzle has fallen into place that proves his innocence and the Drake brothers' guilt.'

Jackson made up his mind. 'OK. They've gone to the line shack at Simmons Creek. Do you know where that is?'

'I know where Simmons Creek is, yes.' Amy nodded. 'The shack shouldn't be hard to find. It won't take us long. I'll go and saddle two horses.'

'Wait.' Jackson caught her arm before she could leave the jailhouse. 'Let a few more people get off the streets first.'

'Why?' Amy was anxious to be on her way, wanted to find out for herself how Tom was.

'It'll be safer that way and a couple of hours more can't make any difference.'

'The marshal is right,' Neil added. 'Mr Cobb and Steadman ain't going anywhere.'

Amy nodded reluctant agreement.

'I promise we'll go as soon as we can.'

21

In a fury, Allan Drake strode away from the livery stable. He'd made a fool of himself and he didn't like that. Reggie was the fool in the family not him!

He'd threatened Amy, his darling Amy, hurt her, been bested by a kid and worse, much worse, blurted out that he loved Amy. He knew she loved him back, even though her face had expressed surprise at his words, but that was only because the kid was there and she felt unable to reveal her feelings in front of him. Of course, sooner or later he would have had to tell her so they could be married. But he certainly hadn't wanted to do it in such a way in such surroundings, or with someone else present. He'd imagined they would confess their love for one another in the hotel dining-room or in the shade of some cottonwoods. Somewhere nice!

His only excuse for his actions was that he was so het up by Tom Steadman escaping justice that he couldn't help himself. Well, he grinned, not justice exactly because Steadman was innocent. But after all the hard work he and Reggie had done, Steadman should have hanged. That way it would be over by now. They could have moved in on Bannister's land and he could move in on Amy.

Now it had all gone wrong. How to put it right?

★　★　★

Fred Warren drew his sons away from the plaza into the relative quiet of one of the side streets.

'We're going home,' he declared.

'Oh, Pa, no!' a chorus of disagreement from Peter and David.

'Yeah. Things might get ugly. I don't want any of you caught up in a fight that ain't nothing to do with us.'

'It is to do with us,' Peter objected.

'It's about Steadman who killed Ralph Bannister.'

'You heard what the marshal said. Steadman might be innocent. If he is then he shouldn't be hanged for something he didn't do. And if he's guilty, Jackson has promised he will hang eventually.'

'If you can believe Marshal Jackson!' Peter said derisively.

'Well, I do. Don't you want the real killer caught and punished?'

Peter and David glanced at one another; of course they did. And while they were certain of Steadman's guilt, others obviously weren't. Who was right?

'Martin needs to get home.' Warren looked at his middle son, who still looked white and ill. 'And your ma will be worried about us all.'

'I want to stay,' Peter said. 'Don't worry, Pa, I'll keep out of trouble I promise. I'll stay away from the saloons. But I need to know what's happening. Pa, I know you didn't like Ralph much and I know he could be ornery when he liked but dammit he was my friend. I owe it to him to keep an eye on things and make sure that someone is brought to justice for his murder.'

'It might be a few days before Jackson hears anything from the judge. Where will you stay?'

'I can sleep in the livery stables. I'll be all right. I'll be careful and I'll come home as soon as everything is worked out.'

Warren could see his eldest son had made up his mind and reluctantly he admitted that Peter was too old to be made to obey his father. Peter was no longer a boy, he was a young man and should be treated as such.

'What about you, David?'

'I'll go with you and Martin, Pa.' David wanted to see justice done, but he had no wish to wait around in Newberry with nothing to do. And he liked his home comforts too much to want to sleep in a stable! 'You don't need me, Peter, do you?'

'No.'

'All right. Let's get the buckboard. We'll see you later, Peter.'

Peter stood and watched them go.

★　★　★

'You did what?' Reggie looked at his brother with incredulous eyes. 'You damn fool.'

'OK, OK, don't go on.'

It had taken Allan sometime to track down his brother. He'd started in the brothel. Of course he wasn't interested in any of the girls who worked there because his heart belonged to Amy. To his surprise Reggie wasn't with any of them. He wasn't in Chadwin's saloon either, probably because that was full of farmers. Eventually he'd found him in the First Choice saloon, a place Reggie usually shunned as too refined. Reggie was drinking alone, with most people giving him a wide berth.

Allan had bought them both whiskey and then confessed.

'You're always telling me to be careful and now look what you've done.' It wasn't often Reggie got the upper hand with Allan and he was determined to make the most of this. At the same time he was worried. They were so close to success and Allan's actions might mean a setback.

'Look, I'm sorry. I never meant it to happen.' Allan bashed a hand down on the table. 'And while I know she'll forgive me I certainly never meant to hurt Miss Mallory. But it happened and it can't be undone.'

Reggie nodded. He decided to say no more; Allan could be pushed so far and no further. 'The question now is what shall we do?'

'Perhaps there's nothing we need do.'

'What d'you mean?'

'I admit I was upset but I've been giving it some thought.' With whiskey warming his stomach Allan was becoming braver and more confident by the minute. 'Just because I told Miss Mallory how I felt it doesn't really mean anything, does it? I love her. How is anyone, any of these dumb townspeople, going to connect that with Bannister's death and Steadman's hanging?'

'You don't think they'll suspect we've been responsible for all that's been happening around here?'

'Reggie, I ask you. Can you see Marshal Jackson coming up with the truth? Or Cobb come to that? How can we get into trouble for my one mistake?'

Reggie thought about that and agreed. As far as he was concerned he and Allan were cleverer and sharper than any other person in Newberry. He smiled.

'What about Steadman? I'd like to see him dead.'

'Me, too, but he ain't here. He could be anywhere. We'll find him eventually and then he'll die. But in the meantime let's have another drink and then get on home.'

'OK.'

Feeling better, Allan watched Reggie

go up to the bar. He might have made a fool of himself but Amy would soon forget about that and come to love him. They were meant for one another. And he was determined that they'd soon be together.

* * *

It wasn't long before Jackson decided the streets were empty enough for Neil and Amy to leave town. Most people had either gone home or drifted down to the saloons. Amy was pleased. She was anxious to be on her way before Greg came back to the jailhouse and tried to stop her going.

'We'll be safe enough' she said, thinking Jackson still had doubts. 'Come on, Neil.' She left the jailhouse before the marshal could change his mind.

Together they walked quickly down to the livery stable. Neil caught up two horses from the corral and Amy helped him saddle and bridle them.

They mounted and rode out into the street.

'Lead on, Miss Mallory.'

Her heart lifting, she would soon see Tom, Amy urged her horse forward.

★   ★   ★

'Hey, look.' Reggie Drake nudged his brother. They had turned the corner by the feed and grain store, just as Neil and Amy rode away. 'Who's that with Miss Mallory? Where are they off to?'

Allan recognized the kid who had interfered in his talk with Amy. His eyes narrowed. 'They're going to wherever it is that damn Cobb has got Steadman hidden.'

'Do you think so? How do you know?'

'I don't *know* for sure, but I bet I'm right.' Allan's heart twisted with hate and anger. Wherever his Amy and the kid were going they shouldn't be riding along together, alone. It wasn't right. The kid would have to be punished for it. 'Reggie, this could be our best chance to settle everything.' They could kill Steadman and Cobb, and the damn kid, and then he could comfort Amy.' 'Let's follow them. Seize our chances.'

'Now you're talking!' Reggie slapped his brother on the back. 'You wait here, watch the direction they take, while I go and get our horses.' He broke into a run.

* * *

Peter Warren was obeying the promise he'd made to his father not to go down to the saloons. He was sticking close to the jail because he thought that was where the answers to who had killed Bannister and what the law was going to do about it would be. When Neil and Amy came out he decided to follow them. He saw them ride out of town and the Drake brothers hurrying after them. He was worried. What were the Drakes doing? He didn't know much about the two brothers but as they were ranchers he didn't trust them. After some deliberation he went back to the jail and told Marshal Jackson what he'd seen.

'Damn!' Jackson swore several times. 'Are you sure?'

Peter nodded.

'When was this?'

' 'Bout thirty minutes ago. Perhaps longer.'

'And you've only now decided to tell me?'

Peter went red. 'I didn't know what to do. I'm sorry. Do the Drakes mean them and Steadman harm?'

'Yeah.'

'Why?'

'Why do they mean them all harm? Because, Peter, they're the damn murderers!'

Jackson paced round his office a few times, wondering what to do. Cobb was a good man, probably able to handle most every situation, but he wouldn't expect that the Drake brothers would be following along after Neil. And the three men might feel hampered by the presence of Amy Mallory. He made up his mind.

'I'll have to go after 'em, see if I can warn Cobb and Steadman before the Drakes find out where they are.'

He went to the door and opened it to be confronted by a short, sturdy man with bristling beard and bristling eyes, whose whole body bristled with anger.

'Judge Bowyer!' he said in a faint voice.

'Jackson!' The judge barrelled his way into the office.

'How did you get here? We haven't received a telegram.'

'That's because the damn line is out. I've had to ride here by horseback, something I haven't done for years, because of the seriousness of the situation. Yes, Mr Jackson, the seriousness of what you've agreed to do. Bellington's might be a good detective agency but its detectives aren't above the law. And neither are you. So, now, I want to know why you've flouted my

223

decision! The decision of the court. If you can't come up with a good enough reason I'll not only have your badge, I'll fling you in jail!'

'But I was just going . . . ' Jackson said helplessly.

'You're not going anywhere before you explain yourself! If you can.'

Jackson knew better than to argue. Judge Bowyer had a reputation for doing exactly what he said. His position as marshal was already in jeopardy from the town council without annoying the judge even more than he already was. He turned to Peter. 'Will you ride after Neil and Miss Mallory?'

'All right.'

'They're at Simmons Creek. And, Peter, don't let the Drakes see you and don't do anything yourself. Just warn Cobb if you can.' Jackson watched him hurry away, thinking that there was no way Peter would catch Neil and Amy up in time.

22

'You ain't strong on not doing anything are you?' Steadman said with a grin as Cobb yet again checked the time on his watch then walked to the door of the shack to look out at the empty landscape. 'It's surely something you should have learned by now.'

'Well, I haven't,' Cobb said shortly. He was in a bad mood. 'I keep wondering about what's happening in Newberry and thinking of all the things that can go wrong.' He came to a halt and stood rigid in the doorway.

'What's up?'

'It damn well looks as if something has gone wrong already. Here come two riders. One of them's Neil. Who's that with him?'

Steadman elbowed him out of the way. Then he smiled. 'It's all right, it's Amy.' He smiled again as Amy saw him and waved. 'Perhaps it means something has actually gone right? Perhaps they've heard from the judge or . . . ' He stopped in mid-sentence. 'What's that?'

'What?'

'Over there.' Steadman pointed towards the hills. 'I thought I saw some sort of movement.'

'Hell yes!' Cobb's sharp eyes spotted two more riders, coming up fast, unseen and unheard by either Neil or Amy. 'Hell, it's the Drakes!'

'Oh God! No.'

'Neil!' Cobb yelled in warning. 'Watch out! Get off your horses!'

Neil was startled but he'd worked with Cobb long enough now to act quickly and then ask questions. Even as there was the bang of a gun he was pushing Amy out of the saddle and jumping down after her.

'Who is it?' Amy asked, from where she had fallen. 'What's happening?'

'I don't know. Keep down.' Neil flung himself on top of her, shielding her body with his own.

At the same time two riders galloped towards them. With a sinking heart Neil recognized Allan and Reggie. How had he not known the two men were following them? He'd stared at their trail several times but the Drakes must have kept well back and kept to the little cover there was. Now they were here! And he and Amy were trapped out in the open.

Reggie was the one doing the firing. The bullets landed all round them with spouts of earth and grit. Neil glanced towards the shack. Steadman was running towards them but he'd never make it in time to help. Cobb emerged from the doorway, rifle in his hands. Neil looked back at the Drake brothers. Would Cobb shoot in time? He was a good shot but he was quite a distance away. He might miss.

Then Allan shouted, 'Mind Amy. Don't hurt Amy.'

A little way away Reggie pulled his horse to a halt and shot at Steadman instead.

Steadman skidded to a halt and Amy screamed as he dropped to the ground.

'He's not hurt,' Neil told her, hoping he was right. He took advantage of the lull in the shooting to draw his own gun. He sent several shots towards Allan and Reggie.

'Amy, darling, come to me,' Allan called. 'You know you love me.'

'Go to hell,' she called back. 'I don't even like you! It's Tom I love. And always will.'

Allan raised his hands and screamed out with horror and fury. 'Nooo! Amy, no!'

Laughing wildly, knowing his brother wouldn't stop him again, Reggie dug spurs into his horse's sides and rode towards Neil and Amy, firing as he came.

'Amy!' Steadman cried, leaping to his feet.

In the shack's doorway Cobb levered the rifle, raised it and aimed carefully.

Even as Reggie was bearing down on Neil and Amy, would ride right over them, Cobb fired. The bullet struck Reggie in the chest, knocking him backwards out of the saddle. With a surprised look on his face as if he couldn't understand how this was happening to him, he landed with a heavy thump near Neil. He moaned several times before he died.

'Reggie!' Allan yelled. He dismounted, his face and voice turning ugly. 'Amy, if I can't have you no one else will.' He clawed at his holster, then looked down in surprise. It was empty.

'Looking for this?' Amy pulled the man's gun out from where it was still stuck in the band of her skirt.

'Don't shoot! Please. No.'

'Don't,' Neil said, grabbing at Amy's arm. 'There's no need.'

She struggled away from him, raised the gun . . . but suddenly Steadman arrived. He bashed into Allan Drake, drew back his arm and punched the man so hard on the jaw that Allan was knocked out completely cold. With a cry, Amy dropped the gun and jumped up, running over to Steadman.

'Tom!'

'Are you OK? All of you?' Cobb raced up.

Quickly he made sure Reggie was dead then went over to Allan, securing the still unconscious man's hands behind him with handcuffs.

'Yeah.' Somewhat shakily Neil got to his feet. 'I think so.'

'What happened? Why are you here? What did Drake mean?'

'About Amy? He thought he loved her. That was the main reason he wanted to blame Steadman for shooting Bannister.'

'Of course.' Cobb smiled. 'I said there was more behind all this than water rights!' He glanced across at Steadman and Amy who were hugging one another as if they'd never let go. 'Oh hell, now who's this?'

Another rider was galloping towards them.

'It's Peter Warren,' Steadman said. He stepped away from Amy, ready for trouble from the young farmer.

Peter called out a greeting and jumped from his horse. 'I've been trying to catch you up,' he said breathlessly to Neil. 'To warn you about the Drakes following you. But I lost my way.' He glanced at Reggie who lay dead on the ground and then at Allan who was sitting up, groaning. 'Are they really the ones killed Ralph?'

Cobb nodded.

'I'll get you for this, all of you,' Allan moaned. 'I'm better than all of you. How dare you. I'll never be found guilty.'

'Oh shut up,' Steadman told him. 'You've lost. Accept it like a man.'

'Where's Jackson?' Cobb demanded. 'Why didn't he come after Neil and Miss Mallory?' The marshal knew the area well, he wouldn't have become lost.

'Sir,' Peter turned to him, 'he couldn't.' He grinned.

'Why not?'

'Because when I left him he was trying to explain matters to Judge Bowyer.'

'The judge has actually arrived in Newberry?'

'He'd just ridden in.'

'Thank God.' Cobb was relieved.

Bowyer must have got his message and decided to act upon it.

'He wasn't very pleased.'

'Then we'd better get on back and help Jackson.' Cobb looked at Steadman and Amy who were once again hugging close and at Allan who looked both furious and close to tears. The man certainly had lost everything: ranch, brother and Amy.

'Neil.'

'Yes, sir?'

'You and Peter fetch the horses. We'll load Reggie on one and Allan on another. Go back to town. Sort this out once and for all.'

Travelling to Oregon, drifter Ryan had taken a job in the new railroad's Montana timber camp. But he fled when company men killed his friend Ben Comfrey over owed wages of seventy-four dollars fifty . . . Ryan knew that Ben's widow and son needed that money to get them through the winter — but when he confronted the railroad bosses, they tried to kill him too. Now, with a capable gun and vengeance in mind, Ryan was going to pursue it to the end of the line.